It was Fatso, together with two of his cronies, Des Davies and Jason Lang, who approached Polly and me at morning break of the day following the theft.

'You fancy yourself as a bit of a sleuth, don't you, James Bond?' was his opening gambit.

I smiled modestly.

'I have had one or two successes – as you know.'

'So I want you to find who nicked my Walkman,' said Fatso briefly.

I gave him a cold stare.

'You mean, bring the thief to justice?'

'I don't give a damn about justice,' retorted Fatso. 'All I know is, if I don't get that Walkman back, Dad's gonna kill me.'

'So what's in it for me?' I said.

There was an awkward sort of silence.

JB Invincible

Jo Dane

RED FOX

A Red Fox Book

Published by Random House Children's Books
20 Vauxhall Bridge Road, London SW1V 2SA

A division of Random House UK Ltd
London Melbourne Sydney Auckland
Johannesburg and agencies throughout the world

First published as 'J.B. VIGILANTE' in 1992
by Hutchinson Children's Books

Red Fox edition 1993

Printed and bound in Great Britain by
Cox & Wyman Ltd, Reading, Berkshire

RANDOM HOUSE UK Limited Reg. No. 954009

ISBN 0 09 921461 X

Contents

JB INVINCIBLE

1
The Elwich Vigilantes

You wouldn't think that taking part in a Neighbour-hood Watch scheme could lead anyone into the most deadly peril, would you? It can. It did.

I suppose that statement's shoving you in at the deep end, isn't it? So perhaps I ought to start by telling you something about myself in case you haven't heard of any of my previous adventures.

First of all, my name is Bond. James Bond. Yes, I know. You'd think parents would be more careful. I'm afraid I'm not a glam type like my famous 007 namesake (spots, spectacles and being small for your age don't make for charm) but I sure do resemble him in other ways, because I keep getting involved in all sorts of thrilling adventures. The name is an awful embarrassment, however, and people do tend to take the mickey, so my mates usually just call me JB.

I live with my family near the small market town of Elwich, where Mum, who has the organizing ability of Cecil B de Mille, runs us, the house and the local WI. My dad works in Camcaster, our nearest industrial town and Susan, my drippy older sister, is away at university studying archaeology, so we hardly see her.

There are three of us in my gang. I'm Boss Man, of course, and my first lieutenant is Paul Perkins, known to all and sundry as Polly. I live in Sycamore Road, while his pad's just round the corner in Laurel Grove. We're also in the same class at Moorside Comprehensive School. He's a bit taller than me and palish, with freckles instead of spots. You can think of him as being like Dr Watson to my Sherlock Holmes whenever we take on the underworld, as we quite frequently do.

Then there's our 'third man' – Sam. Sam's a girl actually, Samantha Spencer. She lives right next door to me and her dad's a cop. Not just the common uniformed kind, mind you. He's one of the plain clothes mob – a detective inspector. He's teaching me judo and he's dead good. Even though Sam's only a girl and a year younger than Polly and me, I have to admit she's a great third man. I hate to say it, but she's far better at judo than I am and, though she's only tiny, she sure is tough and has the stamina of Anneka Rice. Bossy with it too. You have to watch her or she'd take over the whole caboodle.

Still, the three of us make a pretty good team and we've had quite a few successes as detectives. This is good practice for me as I aim to become Assistant Commissioner at Scotland Yard when I grow up. We all three want a career with a bit of go in it. Sam hankers after being an airline pilot, while Polly's dream is to be a top pathologist.

Talking of our oldies – well, briefly, mine have never heard of children's rights and think all kids should be born aged about thirty, while Polly's are a real couple of fusspots. His mum, for instance, keeps the house so spotless it's the sort of place where even cockroaches would wash their hands.

Anyway, I know you're all dying for me to get on to the exciting stuff, which begins, as I said, with our Neighbourhood Watch scheme.

Sam's dad, being a cop, was instrumental in getting the whole thing off the ground. He'd sent round leaflets to everybody explaining the virtues of such a scheme and finally he'd called a meeting in our Community Centre to discuss it. Polly and Sam and I all went along with our parents. Not because we were invited, mind you, but because our oldies don't like leaving us in the house on our own at night. Carol Anne, Polly's kid sister, didn't come though. She'd gone off to her best friend's birthday party and the friend's parents had heroically volunteered to hang on to her till she was collected. I didn't envy them. Personally, I've had Carol Anne up to *here*. That kid gets up my nose like a Vick's inhaler.

However, to get back to the meeting. A lot of it was dead boring. You know how grown-ups rabbit on about things. But I thought I ought to show an interest. I mean, I've had more experience of solving crimes than anyone else in our neighbourhood, so I reckoned my ideas might be helpful. I should have known better. I did once put my hand up to speak, but the chairman just ignored me and my father shot me one of those looks which could stop traffic in the fast lane of the M1. Finally, when it came to electing a co-ordinator (who would be like a commanding officer) for the area, I hoped I might be offered the job. No such luck. I might have been invisible. Instead they chose Mr Maltravers, the manager of a local building society, an inoffensive type, who looked like an overfed rabbit and was obviously incapable of tackling any armed villain. I was pretty disgusted, I can tell you, and I said as much to Polly while we stood around waiting for our oldies at the end of the meeting.

'I could do that job standing on my head,' I said. 'Look at all the villains we've tackled. I don't suppose that Maltravers guy even knows judo.'

'He won't have to,' said Polly. 'The co-ordinator isn't supposed to *tackle* burglars. He just rings the fuzz and they come and deal with it.'

I gazed at him in horror.

'You mean he's not armed or anything? How wet! Anyone could ring the cops. I thought he'd head a posse or—'

Polly shook his head.

'No, JB. You're thinking of the Guardian Angels. You know – like on the London Underground. Neighbourhood Watch isn't like that.'

'So what *do* they do?'

'Watch,' said Polly simply.

'We ought to start our own scheme.' Sam, who'd been listening, decided to put her oar in. 'Maybe something with a bit more go in it.'

I hesitated. Sam may be only a girl, but she does have the odd brill idea and she's game for anything. All the same, I didn't want to sound too eager. I'm Number One Man in our gang and it doesn't do to let the others forget it.

'You may have something there,' I said judiciously. 'I'll have a think and see what I come up with.'

4

Sam gave me a scornful look and opened her mouth for a scathing reply. But we were collected by our respective oldies at this point so the conversation was shelved.

It was Polly who solved the problem a day or two later.

The two of us were cycling home from school as usual, feeling on top of the world because it was the last day before our February half term holiday and a whole glorious week of freedom stretched ahead of us. Suddenly Polly, with the air of Einstein announcing his latest theory to the world, said, 'We're in Elm Drive now.'

I tried glaring at him, but the traffic got in the way.

'I know that, you moron. We come this way every day.'

'Elm Drive,' persisted Polly, 'hasn't got a Neighbourhood Watch scheme.'

'So?'

'So I thought we might guard Elm Drive,' said Polly simply. 'Just to watch, you know. Nothing dangerous,' he added hastily.

'Hang on!' I braked so suddenly Polly almost ran into me. 'You sure about this?'

'Positive.' Polly dismounted and leaned his bike against a lamppost. I remained standing straddled across my mount. 'I heard Dad saying so only last night. They couldn't get anyone interested, he said. So I thought—'

'You'll do yourself an injury,' I said sarcastically. 'It's not a bad idea though. Give us something to do over the holiday. Dad's always on at me about spending leisure time positively. Park your bike and let's have a recce.'

We leaned our bikes against someone's garden fence and began to walk slowly down the street. I was eyeing all the houses carefully.

'JB?' questioned Polly.

'Yeah?'

'What're we looking for?'

I stared at him coldly.

'To see if anyone's got Neighbourhood Watch stickers in the window, of course. Your dad could be wrong, you know. It's been known.'

Polly looked a bit reproachful at this, but, when we had walked slowly up and down the street on each side without finding a single Neighbourhood Watch notice, I began to think his dad must be right for once and said as much.

'Told you so!' muttered Polly rebelliously.

'Yeah, well. I was just making sure. OK then. We'll adopt Elm Drive. We'll start in the morning.'

'Are we telling Sam?'

'Not yet,' I said. 'We'll see how it goes.'

Ten o'clock next morning, therefore, found us turning into Elm Drive on foot and alert for anything suspicious. After giving the matter some thought I had dressed for the part. I was wearing dark sunlenses clipped on to my specs and an old camouflage jacket I'd nicked from our Susan's wardrobe. Honestly, that girl goes around looking like she gets her gear from an Oxfam closing down sale. Still, I felt the jacket was just right for this job and I'd managed to sneak it out of the house without Mum noticing. Polly had made only one con-

6

cession to the job in hand. Round his neck was slung a rather fine pair of binoculars. He was obviously taking the watching idea pretty seriously. Also, I reckoned that as his mum always provided him with a large, clean hanky before he left the house, he could use that as a half mask if necessary.

Disappointingly, the street seemed as quiet and law-abiding as even the most nervous citizen could wish. An elderly woman was brushing the flagstones in front of her gate; a small girl pedalled a small bike along the pavement; two women gossiped over the front hedge and the odd pedestrian ambled aimlessly down the street. It's not a particularly busy road at the best of times, but a few cars passed, all carefully obeying the 30 mph limit. Not a lawbreaker of any sort in sight.

There were several vehicles parked in the street and I suddenly remembered a remark Detective Inspector Spencer had made in his talk a few nights previously:

'Strange cars parked outside your house may be suspicious. Note the number. If the car remains there for any length of time, particularly if it is occupied, report it.'

'Let's have a dekko at the parked cars,' I said.

'Shall I note the numbers, JB?' Polly was beginning to enter into the spirit of the thing.

'Yeah. Do that,' I said.

We strolled along the street, with me peering into all the cars and Polly laboriously writing the numbers at the back of his diary. Only two of the cars were occupied. In the first, a small white poodle objected loudly when I pressed my face against the glass. Farther down the street a shadowy figure sitting behind the wheel of a blue Ford Sierra slid lower in the seat as we approached, holding a newspaper up before his face.

'See that?' I hissed at Polly as soon as we got past.

'See what?' said Polly blankly.

'The bloke in the blue Ford. No! Don't turn round, moron. He didn't want to be seen.'

'How d'you know?'

'Because he held up his paper to hide his face when he saw me looking at the cars. I reckon he's a crook.'

'Gosh!' said Polly. There was a pause while his brain creaked into gear, then he made his usual contribution to the conversation.

'What shall we do, JB?'

I'd been thinking about that one.

'Tell the cops, I s'pose. I mean, that's what Sam's dad said.'

'Oh, fine.' Polly's face cleared. I think he'd suspected I'd want us to arrest the guy ourselves. 'Shall we ring them? The nick's miles away.'

'Good thinking,' I said. 'There's a phone box at the end of the next street. Come on. It's a chance to dial 999.'

We trotted off.

No sooner had we turned out of Elm Drive, however, than we saw a familiar figure cycling down the road towards us.

'Hang on,' I said. 'Isn't that Constable Hoskins?'

'Sure is,' nodded Polly. 'What a bit of luck!'

I galloped across the road to waylay Hoskins.

'Hello Mr Hoskins,' I yelled as I approached. 'Remember me?'

It was obvious that the constable, who had been unwillingly involved in some of our previous cases, did remember and, to judge from his expression, none of the memories were especially happy ones. However, he dismounted, albeit reluctantly, and gave me his full attention.

'James Bond! You again. And Paul something or other – I always forget.'

'Perkins,' said Polly in resigned tones.

'Perkins – that's it. Well, what's wrong this time?'

'We,' I said impressively, 'have seen a man acting suspiciously in Elm Drive.'

Hoskins looked at me blankly.

'In what way? What was he doing?'

'Sitting in a car,' I said.

Hoskins sighed.

'People do sit in cars, James. It's not unusual.'

'It's unusual to try and hide behind a newspaper when you see me coming,' I said triumphantly.

'I know how he felt.' Hoskins spoke with feeling. I scowled at him.

'I think he was casing the joint before breaking in. Inspector Spencer told us to report people sitting around in cars. Anyway, it's a blue Ford Sierra.'

'Number E174 OFM,' supplied Polly.

'And it's been there quite a bit. Outside number eighteen it is. And—'

'Ah!' said Constable Hoskins. 'Right, lads. Fine. Leave it to me now. I'll see to it.' For some reason he seemed suddenly edgy.

I looked at him suspiciously.

9

'You will do something?'

'Right away.' Hoskins was already producing his walkie-talkie. 'You two cut along home now. And thanks for letting me know.'

'That's OK,' I said and stood hopefully by him, so I could correct his account to headquarters if he got it wrong.

Constable Hoskins, however, seemed reluctant to make his report in my presence. He eyed me balefully.

'Off you go, I said.'

He was beginning to sound quite agitated. Polly clutched my sleeve.

'Come on, JB.'

'OK,' I said. 'This way.'

'But that's—'

'Come on!' I hissed, giving him a shove. Polly obeyed.

'Aren't we going home then?' he said, once we were out of earshot.

'Not likely,' I said. 'We're going back to Elm Drive to see what happens.'

We scurried along the road and turned into Elm Drive.

'The car's still there,' reported Polly.

'Well, the police won't have had time to act yet,' I said. 'You know what cops are like. Have to fill in half a dozen forms first. I wonder if they'll come armed? He might be dangerous.'

'They're going to be too late anyway,' said Polly in disappointment.

Halfway down the street the blue Sierra was edging cautiously out of the line of parked cars. A

10

minute later it had driven off in the opposite direction, turned a corner and disappeared from view.

'Typical!' I said bitterly. 'Just typical. We go to all that trouble and the cops don't even hurry. Let's hang around and see how long it takes them.'

We spent fifteen boring minutes hanging about in that rotten street. No police cars appeared.

'Shall we leave it, JB?' said Polly at last.

That's the trouble with Polly. Everybody else's staying power is so much better quality.

'Let's just walk down the street again,' I said. 'Try to see what he was watching or waiting for.'

I set off. Polly sighed, but followed me reluctantly.

We passed the empty place where the car had been. All seemed peaceful. Suddenly Polly clutched my arm.

'JB – there's someone moving in that house.'

I looked at him blankly.

'Well, of course. People live there.'

'N-no.' Polly was beginning to stammer as he always does when he's excited or scared. 'N-not that one. The empty house. Opposite us. N-number twenty-five.'

I looked. Number twenty-five was obviously empty. A FOR SALE board flapped desolately by the broken front gate. The windows were grimy and uncurtained. The whole place looked run down and dejected. There was no sign of life.

'What exactly did you see?' I said disbelievingly.

'A flash of light.' Polly sounded quite definite. 'In one of the b-bedrooms. The smaller one over the

11

garage. It looked like the sun caught a b-bit of glass or something.'

I looked at the window he indicated. And after a moment—

'You're right,' I said excitedly. 'There's someone up there. So that's what the bloke in the car was doing. He's their lookout man. They're up to something in that house.'

'Gosh!' said Polly in awe. His vocabulary really is pretty limited. 'Shall we go after Hoskins and tell him?'

I frowned.

'We need hard evidence, don't we? That's what the cops always say. Hard evidence.'

Polly looked doubtful.

'So how do we get it?'

I was thinking rapidly.

'That room where the light flashed. It's the bedroom over the garage. Right?'

'Right,' repeated Polly obediently.

'And that room goes right through to the back and another window overlooks the back garden. Right?'

'Right,' came my echo.

'So let's get round to the back', I said. 'If we go on up the road we'll come to the alley between the houses, won't we?'

'That just leads on to fields,' said Polly.

'Exactly,' I said triumphantly. 'And the fields are at the back of these houses. So come on. Count the houses we pass.'

'Why?'

'So we know when we're behind number twenty-five, moron.'

'We're bound to know.' Polly was showing signs of rebellion. 'It's the only one empty.'

We scuttled down the alley and on to the open fields.

Behind number twenty-five a low wooden fence separated the large, unkempt garden from the fields. Just the other side of the fence a big oak tree overhung the neglected lawn. I clutched Polly's arm.

'See that tree?'

'It's an oak tree,' said Polly helpfully.

'I know that, you thicko. If we climbed it we could see into that room, couldn't we? With your binoculars we could. Easy.'

Polly hesitated.

'I don't like it, JB. There was nothing said at that meeting about getting into people's gardens and climbing trees. It's trespassing.'

'Oh, don't be such a wimp,' I snapped. 'Come on.'

The fence was quite easy to climb. Polly, still wittering away agitatedly, followed me over it. I eyed the tree.

'Plenty of footholds,' I said triumphantly. 'Piece of cake.'

I began to scramble ungracefully up the gnarled trunk. I didn't bother to look back to see if Polly was following. I knew he would. He may be thick and he may have no head for heights, but he's loyal.

We perched in a fork about three quarters of the way up.

'You can see right into the room from here,' I said excitedly. 'Give us the glasses.'

Polly obediently unhooked the binoculars from around his neck and handed them over. I peered through them.

'Everything's blurry.'

'You gotta adjust them,' said Polly. 'Twist that thing. There.'

I obeyed. I still couldn't see much.

'Not much cop are they, these glasses?' I said.

'I think,' said Polly apologetically, 'that you'd see better, JB, if you took your sunglasses off.'

He was right, of course. I'd forgotten I was wearing them. I gave him an irritated glower, but removed the dark lenses from the front of my specs. Then I again put the binoculars to my eyes.

The picture sprang into focus. It was fab. I could see right into that room as clear as anything.

There were two men there, one tallish and heavily built, the other smaller, fair and stocky. The room was still furnished, I noticed. A large built-in wardrobe was against the right hand wall. It was open and the men appeared to be putting things into it. At least . . . . I peered more closely. It might be more correct to say they were putting stuff *through* it. There seemed to be another opening at the back of the wardrobe, but its half-open door partially blocked my vision in a most irritating manner.

'Let's have a dekko,' breathed Polly in my ear.

Reluctantly I handed over the binoculars.

'Look at the back of the wardrobe,' I instructed.

Polly wriggled round to get a better view. I moved farther along my branch. There was an ominous crack. I let out a startled gurgle. Amid a tangle of broken branches I slithered unceremoniously down to land on the lawn below with a bump that temporarily winded me.

'JB!' came Polly's anxious voice from above my head. 'Are you OK?'

I sat up slowly and dizzily. I was just deciding thankfully that I was still in one piece, when the back door of the house opened and the two men rushed out. They looked, I observed blearily, decidedly cross.

From the branches above me I heard Polly give a terrified moan, and before I could collect my senses the smaller man had seized me and yanked me to my feet.

'What d'you think you're up to?' he demanded.

I stared at him in a mesmerized sort of way, like a rabbit eyeing a particularly ill-natured and persistent ferret. The other man was looking up at the tree.

'There's another of 'em up there,' he said. 'Come down out of it, you little devil.'

'C-coming.' Polly scrambled clumsily down and stood beside me.

'Were you spying?' snapped the man holding me. He then proceeded to shake me so violently that I felt my spots cannoning into one another.

'No,' I said hastily. 'Why should we? What is there to spy on?'

'So why were you up there?'

'Just climbing,' I said. 'It looked a good tree. I bet my mate I could get higher than him.'

I was just thinking what a megacool response this

15

was on my part, when I remembered the binoculars. You don't carry binoculars just to climb trees. I should have said we were bird-watchers or something. I darted a hasty glance at Polly. Then I did a double take.

No binoculars were visible. I wondered if they were still in the tree, but I daren't look up in case it gave our captors the idea. Instead I gazed straight at the guy holding me with my innocent-but-not-too-bright expression. He, in turn, looked at his partner who appeared to be in charge.

'What shall we do with 'em, Mike?'

'Bring them inside,' decided the taller man. 'Then we'll see.'

'We've got to get home,' I said desperately. 'We're late as it is.'

Our captors took no notice. We were hustled up the garden and shoved ungently through the back door, which was promptly kicked shut behind us. I felt like the Count of Monte Cristo saying hello to the Chateau d'If.

Once inside, I looked round. We were in the kitchen, I noticed. A grimy, dusty place, but with definite signs of occupation. A kettle stood on the stove and, on a rickety table, were two mugs which had obviously been used. There were also some loose tea bags and a carton of milk.

The taller bloke – Mike – pointed to two wooden chairs at one side of the table.

'Sit!' he commanded.

We sat and eyed him anxiously.

'You were trespassing,' he said accusingly. 'The tree you were climbing was *in* the garden.'

16

'We thought the house was empty,' I said. 'I mean, it looked empty.'

'So you couldn't see in?'

'We didn't look,' I said. 'Why should we? Anyway, it was too far away.'

Our interrogator seemed to relax a bit at that. He eyed us in a considering sort of way, then he said, 'Right, lads. I believe you. Now, it's important that you don't tell anyone you've seen us. Understand?'

'Why?' I said.

The smaller man seemed about to speak, but the other one stopped him.

'We're on a case,' he said impressively. 'We're police officers, see? Flying squad.'

'Cor!' I said. 'Just like in films!'

'Exactly. And we're laying a trap for a bunch of crooks.'

'Gosh!' said Polly, joining in the conversation for the first time.

'What sort of crooks?' I asked. 'Is it drugs or terrorists or—'

'I'm not at liberty to say,' said Mike quickly. 'But it's essential no word of our being here gets out.'

Suddenly everything clicked into place in my mind.

'The crooks could be on to you,' I said. 'There was a blue Ford Sierra parked along the road earlier. The bloke in it was trying to hide behind his paper. He could have been watching the house.'

The smaller man let out a very rude word indeed. His boss shushed him hurriedly and turned back to me.

17

'Is he still there?' he questioned.

'No,' I said. 'He went. We reported him to the cops. To Constable Hoskins actually. He's a pal of ours.'

The smaller man swore again. He really seemed a very excitable type. His superior smiled at me.

'The local police aren't in on this, laddie. It's really big.'

'Can we help?' I asked eagerly.

'Only by keeping your mouths shut. Not a word to anyone or you'll blow our cover.'

I nodded helpfully.

'You can trust us,' I said. 'We won't breathe a word. Will we, Polly?'

Polly shook his head in his usual demented metronome fashion.

The big bloke eyed us closely for a moment, then nodded as if satisfied.

'Right. Good lads. Now scarper – out the way you came. And don't come hanging round here again. D'you hear?'

'Understood,' I said grandly. 'But if you should want any help—'

The man gave a short laugh.

'Thanks, lad. But it's too dangerous. And remember, our lives are in your hands.'

'I'll remember,' I said solemnly, giving him my best honest, open, English hero look. As I turned away I could practically hear the background music reaching a crescendo.

The smaller guy opened the back door and gave a quick glance round, then beckoned us to leave.

We slithered out. The door shut silently behind us.
Polly opened his mouth to speak but I grabbed him.

'Come on.'

We scuttled across the lawn and over the fence.
Once in the field beyond, I turned to Polly.

'What did you do with the binoculars?'

'They're here somewhere.' Polly was scrabbling
about in the long grass. 'I threw them over the fence
when I saw the men come out. I hope they're not
broken. They belong to Dad.'

'Why did you chuck them away?'

'So's they wouldn't know we were spying on
them,' said Polly promptly. 'I thought at first they
were crooks, you see.'

'Yeah. So did I,' I said. 'Good job they weren't.
Still – just as well they don't know we saw what
they were up to.'

'I didn't,' said Polly rebelliously. 'I'd only just
got the glasses when you did your nose dive.'

'Oh – well – they were hiding boxes of stuff and
big flat things in a wardrobe.'

Polly frowned.

'Why would cops do that?'

'I don't know, do I?' I snapped irritably. 'Perhaps
they're laying a trap for the baddies. Come on. Find
those binoculars and let's get out of here.'

'Got them.' Polly made a triumphant grab.
'Great! They're not broken.'

He slung them round his neck.

'Right. Let's go.' I led the way back across the
field and along the alley.

As we emerged into Elm Drive a voice hailed us
and as we turned Sam belted up on her bike and

19

braked sharply to a halt beside us. She eyed us suspiciously.

'What are you two up to?'

'Doing our own version of *Crimewatch*,' I said.

Sam glared at me.

'Without me? You rotten hound. It was my idea.'

'We were going to tell you,' I said placatingly. 'Just wanted to try it out first to see it wasn't a flop.'

Sam relaxed slightly.

'And was it? A flop, I mean?'

'Not exactly,' I said. 'There's certainly something going on, but the cops are on to it. They've told us to keep mum.'

'You can tell me,' said Sam promptly. 'I'm your third man. Remember?'

'Yeah, well, OK.' I capitulated under Sam's steady gaze. Honestly, if you put that girl in the ring with Mike Tyson I'd back her any time. She'd terrorize him into submission. 'You see,' I said, 'first of all, there was this bloke in the car . . . .'

I went carefully through the whole saga. Retold, it began to sound a bit thin really. By the time I'd got to the end my voice gradually died away under Sam's disbelieving stare.

There was a pause. Then Sam spoke.

'I've never heard such a load of codswallop in all my life.'

'You what?' I said weakly.

Polly's mouth opened and shut but no sound came out.

'Don't you see, JB?' Sam sounded impatient. 'You've got it all the wrong way round. The guy in

20

the car was a cop. The crooks were the ones in the house.'

'But they said—'

'What did you expect them to say?' Sam interrupted scornfully. 'Tell you they were villains and up to something? Fancy believing a yarn like that! Call yourself a detective!'

'But—' I began.

Sam overrode any objection I might make.

'If they were cops what were they hiding? The only reason police might be in there would be to keep an eye on the street for some reason. But they weren't doing that, were they?'

'Well – no,' I said. 'But—'

'You let them con you,' said Sam disgustedly. 'You'll never be a proper sleuth if you believe everything any smart aleck tells you.'

I was stung, but worse was to follow. Polly cleared his throat. I swung round on him.

'I think she's right, JB,' he said apologetically. 'I thought it was funny all along.'

I hesitated. I hated to admit it, but it was beginning to look as if Sam might indeed be right. I should have used my deductive powers instead of listening to those two plausible con merchants. There was a bright side though. If I'd not been so eager to go along with them, or shown I didn't believe their story, Polly and I might not be standing here now. We might have been lying bound and gagged on the floor of that wardrobe. I pulled myself together.

'Of course,' I said loftily, 'I was a bit suspicious from the word go.' (Polly looked at me blankly.)

21

'But I had to pretend to go along with them, didn't I? They were quite ruthless. You could see that.'

Sam just stared at me and made the sound that is usually written as 'Huh!'

'So,' I continued hastily, 'we've got to decide what's best to do now. Is your dad at home, Sam?'

Sam shook her head.

'Sacré bleu!' I said. 'We'd better get along to the nick in Elwich then. Though they probably won't believe us.'

'Hang on.' Sam sounded excited. 'Dad said at breakfast he'd be around Elwich all day. If he's there at the nick—'

I looked at her hopefully.

'That'd help. If,' I added bitterly, 'the Gorgons on duty at the desk even let us see him.'

Sam stared at me.

'They'll let *me*. I'm his *daughter*. Come on. Get a move on.' She sprang on her bike.

Polly and I galloped off in pursuit.

The sergeant who appeared at the glass pigeon-hole thing in answer to our ring contemplated us as a spider might contemplate three flies caught in its web.

'Well?'

'Is Detective Inspector Spencer in?' I asked, trying to sound all grown-up and confident.

'He may be,' said the sergeant cautiously. 'Or then again he may not. If he is in, he's busy.'

Sam decided to take a hand.

'Please sir,' she said, using her helpless-little-girl voice, 'he's my daddy. And we must see him. It's ever so urgent. A matter of life and death.'

22

The sergeant looked at her doubtfully.

Girls do have an advantage, you know, in this sort of situation. Sam is small for her age, with blonde hair and large blue eyes. She was wearing her butter-wouldn't-melt expression and looking at that sergeant like he could walk on water.

'Please sir,' she said again.

The sergeant crumbled. I knew he would.

'Hang on, lovey,' he said and picked up the phone.

Five minutes later we were in Detective Inspector Spencer's office.

Sam's dad was looking a bit anxious when we entered. He glanced inquiringly at Sam.

'Anything wrong at home?'

'Not a blind thing,' said Sam happily. 'We just had to see you urgently. James and Polly have been tackling crooks in Elm Drive.'

Mr Spencer began to grin.

'I know,' he said. 'That was me in the car, James. I didn't want you to recognize me and come bounding up. Then Hoskins told me you were snooping around and had reported me as a suspicious character, so I drove off and sent someone else in another car on the job.'

'Oh!' I said flatly. 'You know about the empty house then?'

Inspector Spencer's gaze sharpened.

'What empty house?'

'The one you were watching. Number twenty-five.'

There was a pause.

'Tell me about the empty house, James,' said Inspector Spencer gently.

'Well,' I said, 'these two were hiding the stuff. And then I fell out of the tree and—'

Mr Spencer sighed.

'It's very confusing, James, when you begin a story in the middle and go both ways. In the words of Humpty Dumpty – begin at the beginning, go on till you get to the end and then stop.'

'Oh!' I said. 'Right. Well, after we'd reported you to Constable Hoskins, we went back to Elm Drive to see what was happening . . . . '

I went through the whole story, trying not to miss anything out. Mr Spencer interrupted only once. He said, 'In the wardrobe, you said?'

'Yeah,' I said. 'It was funny, that wardrobe. It was one of those built-in jobs. And it looked like there was another door at the back. But there couldn't have been, could there? Because it would have gone through to next door and—'

'So that's it!' Inspector Spencer slapped his hand sharply on the desk, making us jump. 'All right, James. Go on.'

'Not much more to tell,' I said. 'That was where I fell out of the tree.'

I finished the story, trying to gloss over the fact that I'd been taken in by those smooth talking villains. Sam's dad didn't seem to think it mattered. He was looking quite excited.

'For your information, James,' he said, 'I wasn't watching number twenty-five. I was watching twenty-three next door, where a bloke answering to the description of one you saw is actually living

24

with his wife and family. We went into number twenty-three yesterday with a search warrant. We found nothing. Now I know why.'

'You mean there's a way through from twenty-three to the empty huose?' I said. 'Through the wardrobe?'

'Exactly. James, you're invaluable. I don't know what we'd do without you.'

'Gee, thanks,' I said. 'But what were they hiding?'

'Remember that series of robberies in the Owley Wood area over the past few weeks?'

'Rather!' I said. 'Valuable ornaments nicked, weren't there? And some pictures?'

'That's right. We had a tip-off the stuff was cached somewhere around Elwich and that the family living at number twenty-three knew more than was good for them. But, as I say, when we searched we drew a blank.'

'Some of the stuff I saw could have been pictures,' I said, remembering. 'Big flat things anyway. Are you going to raid 'em now? Can we come?'

'Please, Dad,' pleaded Sam.

Polly gave us a look of horror. To his obvious relief Sam's dad shook his head and rose to his feet.

'Sorry, James. But the answer's no. And I'm afraid I'm going to send you three home pronto. It's going to be all systems go here. Anyway, congratulations on an excellent bit of detection.'

I smiled smugly.

'Any time. No problem,' I told him.

On the pavement outside the nick, Sam turned to me.

'Well,' she said coldly, 'a nice mess you got your-selves into without me. Good job I happened along to sort things out.'

'Hey, steady on!' I said weakly. 'We sussed out the crooks, didn't we?'

'Anything could have happened to you in that house, barging in like that,' Sam retorted. 'You were in deadly danger.'

'D-danger?' Polly's voice came out in a strangled squeak which would have fascinated a throat specialist.

'*Deadly* danger,' repeated Sam firmly. 'Falling out of a tree right into their hands! You were dead lucky to escape. So no more Neighbourhood Watch without me. Right?'

'Right,' I said. 'Next case – you're in. But "Neighbourhood Watch" sounds a bit wimpish, doesn't it? Couldn't we call ourselves something with a bit more zing to it?'

'How about the Elwich Vigilantes?' suggested Polly diffidently.

Sam beamed at him in the way a teacher does to a kid who's just come up with the right answer.

'That's really wicked! Radical! I go for that. What do you say, JB?'

I turned to Polly.

'Spot-on, mate. Elwich Vigilantes it is. We'll be terrific.'

'All three of us,' said Sam firmly.

2
The Moorside Menace

Once we'd formed the Elwich Vigilantes we began to look out for baddies not only in Elm Drive but all over the town. And, of course, just to spite us it seemed, the whole of Elwich appeared to be leading an excessively law-abiding life. We were beginning to think the whole thing was a dead duck when we walked straight into a spot of petty larceny, not in Elm Drive but at Moorside Comprehensive School itself.

We don't get a lot of organized crime at Moorside. Not compared with some of the comprehensives over in Camcaster anyway. This is probably mainly due to three of our top brass, known throughout the school as the 'Unholy Trinity'.

First and foremost is Bonzo Barker, our headmaster. To say he's respected and feared by all is the understatement of the year. He's a guy who looks as if he's been manufactured by the same firm that built Stonehenge and in whom it would be difficult to detect a love of children even with the most delicate instrument.

His second in command is Mrs Wallis, popularly known as the Walrus. Imagine a pit bull terrier in a skirt and you've got the picture.

The third member of this Mafia type alliance is Taff Evans, our very own head of second year. And *he's* a large, hefty, rugger-playing hulk, who makes Rambo look like a toddler.

So as you see, crime, against such powerful forces of law and order, doesn't stand much of a chance.

Everybody was quite surprised, therefore, when soon after the February half term, it became obvious that we had a thief in our midst. A pretty expert one too. A penknife left unguarded on your own desk for no more than two minutes was minus when you returned. PE kit disappeared with monotonous regularity and Fatso Austin, who'd been unwise enough to break the rules by bringing his new Walkman into school, had it nicked the very first day.

It was Fatso, together with two of his cronies, Des Davies and Jason Lang, who approached Polly and me at morning break of the day following the theft.

'You fancy yourself as a bit of a sleuth, don't you, James Bond?' was his opening gambit.

I smiled modestly.

'I have had one or two successes – as you know.'

'So I want you to find who nicked my Walkman,' said Fatso briefly.

I gave him a cold stare.

'You mean, bring the thief to justice?'

'I don't give a damn about justice,' retorted Fatso. 'All I know is, if I don't get that Walkman back, Dad's gonna kill me.'

'So what's in it for me?' I said.

There was a awkward sort of silence. That I should want a reward for my services had obviously never crossed Fatso's pure mind. But his dad, who's a long-distance lorry driver, is known by all to have a pretty uncertain temper, to put it mildly. If Fatso were to survive, it was essential he recovered that Walkman before his father's next arrival home. After a pause, he said tentatively, 'A quid?'

'Peanuts!' I countered. 'Make it five.'

'A fiver?' squeaked Fatso. 'That's a bit steep. My pocket money for a month, that is.'

'I've got expenses,' I said loftily. 'Take it or leave it.'

Fatso was desperate enough to capitulate. I knew he would be.

'OK,' he said glumly. 'Payment strictly by results, of course.'

'Eh?' I said.

'If you don't find who's nicking the stuff you get zilch,' he translated.

'That's fair,' agreed his sidekicks, in threatening tones.

'OK,' I said. 'No problem.'

We went into class.

Polly and Sam and I discussed the matter on the way home from school that afternoon, walking our bikes along the pavement as we usually did when we had some weighty problem to solve.

'I don't think you should have agreed to take the case.' Polly, spreading gloom and despondency as usual, made his contribution as soon as I'd put Sam in the picture.

'Five quid's not to be sneezed at,' I said.

'That's only if you get the Walkman back. And if Bonzo and Taff and the Walrus between them are stymied, what chance have *you* to find the culprit?'

'I've had more experience of crime,' I said.

'But it could be *anyone*,' said Polly. 'What hope—'

'Not anyone,' interrupted Sam. 'The only kids who've had stuff nicked are second years. Right? So the thief's likely to be one of your own year.'

I thought about that one. She was right, of course. It figured. Though it was a fact which, up to now, I'd overlooked.

I nodded gravely.

'I was wondering if you'd spot that. Yes, that limits the field at once, of course.'

'Only to about 150 kids,' said Polly bitterly.

'Yeah – well – something'll turn up. You'll see.'

Something did turn up only a couple of days later – something we'd never even considered as a possibility.

The thief nicked Polly's new trainers.

Polly's oldies, as I've already mentioned, are a couple of doting fusspots. Nothing's too good for their son. So when Polly hinted to them that he yearned for a pair of Reebok trainers, his mum wasted no time in trotting out to buy them for him. Sam and I, whose parents are neither millionaires nor pushovers for a sob story, were green with envy.

Polly swanned round the place for three whole days in those Reeboks before they were nicked.

It all happened so simply too. We'd gone across to the Arts block for Drama with Miss Holmes that afternoon. Before we're allowed to enter the Drama studio we have to remove our shoes and socks and leave them in a neat row in the foyer. Any stranger visiting the school could be pardoned for thinking he was about to enter a mosque. Anyway, Polly tucked his socks into his Reeboks and left them by my plebeian pair of track shoes. Then we both went into the forty minutes of disorganized chaos that appears on our timetable as Drama.

When the bell went at the end of the lesson we all charged out as usual and dived for our shoes and socks. Only Polly's weren't there. His socks lay forlornly in the space between my shoes and a pair belonging to a shy, self-effacing lad called Peter Stanton.

'My trainers!' Polly's voice rose a couple of decibels. 'JB, someone's nicked my trainers!'

'They can't have,' I said.

'So where are they?' Polly demanded belligerently.

I looked round. The rest of the mob were busy shoving their feet into shoes and socks. No spare footgear was visible. I raised my voice.

'Anyone seen Polly's trainers?'

There were immediate denials. Fatso Austin said, 'That nutter'll have nicked 'em. Perhaps now you'll make more effort to nail him.'

I glowered across at him.

'I'm doing all I can. You didn't give me much to go on, you know. These things take time.'

Fatso sniffed.

'Wonder how many more people've got to lose stuff before you get your act together.'

Polly had been racing round like a demented gazelle, doing a disorganized sort of search of the foyer. He slid to a halt beside me.

'They're n-not here. Anywhere.'

'You'd better tell Miss.' Sharon Mills, whose

31

dad's a cop, came up with the usual popular idea of passing the buck to a higher authority.

'I suppose so.' I spoke without enthusiasm. Miss Holmes, commonly known as 'Jingle Bells' because of the amount of jewellery she wears, is not really efficient even at teaching. In a crisis situation such as this, I feared an appeal to her would be about as much use as throwing an aspirin to a drowning man.

I was right.

'Are you sure that's where you left them?' she bleated ineffectually when she'd heard our tale of woe.

Polly and I assured her this was the case.

'Oh dear!' She eyed us helplessly before sending off to request help from a still higher power.

This power, in the form of Taff Evans, arrived looking like a thundercloud on the loose. He immediately instituted a search of all the class, lining up the boys in front of him and the girls, wittering agitatedly, in front of Jingle Bells, who was exhibiting symptoms of blind panic.

No trainers.

'Anyone in school could have taken them,' Taff said bitterly at last. 'Did you think to lock the outer door, Miss Holmes?'

Miss Holmes shook her head mutely.

'I thought not.' Taff gave a long-suffering sigh. 'Paul, is your name in the trainers?'

Polly hastily assured him this was the case.

'Well, that's something,' said Taff, in tones which implied it wasn't much. 'I'll do another check at home time. If that doesn't find them I'll tell everyone in assembly tomorrow that I'm calling in the police. Now, you'd better come with me and I'll find you some shoes to wear.'

He swept off. Polly followed glumly, to return about ten minutes later – when the rest of us had settled down to Geography – slopping along in a disreputable pair of canvas shoes Taff had acquired from the lost property box.

At the end of afternoon school, when Polly was still moaning agitatedly about his loss and about the probable reaction of his mum, we encountered Sam in the bike shed. She took one quick look at our faces and inquired, 'What's up?'

We explained. Sam looked thoughtful.

'Looks like it's one of your own form,' she said.

'How come?' I said. 'Anyone could have got in and nicked 'em while we were in the studio.'

'Yeah. But it's not likely, is it? Someone just going past tries the door, finds it unlocked and comes in on the off chance there's something worth nicking? Nah. It's someone who's green with envy and who knows he takes the SAME SIZE IN SHOES!'

'Gosh!' said Polly in amazement. 'Sometimes, Sam, you're *awesome*.'

I scowled.

'Yeah. Well – I was thinking along those lines myself.'

'So who,' Sam said, ignoring my attempt to grab the limelight, 'went out of the studio for any reason during the drama session?'

I thought back. Inspiration came.

'Des Davies,' I said triumphantly. 'Said he felt sick. He was out quite a bit.'

33

'There you are then,' said Sam with finality. 'There's your thief.'

'Hang on a sec,' Polly sounded puzzled. 'You reckon whoever nicked my Reeboks also nicked Fatso's Walkman and the other stuff?'

I nodded.

'Figures, doesn't it? There's not *dozens* of baddies around. This is Moorside not Wormwood Scrubs.'

'But Des Davies,' said Polly stubbornly, 'is Fatso's best mate.'

'So what?' said Sam.

'Well – so he wouldn't nick Fatso's Walkman. Would he?'

I thought about that one.

'He might,' I said at last. 'He's shifty. You can see that. I mean, his eyes are so close together you could hardly stick a pin between them. D'you know what size shoes he takes?'

'Gosh!' Polly's eyes widened in horror. 'Same as me. I know because only yesterday he asked if he could try my trainers on. Said his oldies were thinking of getting some for him.'

'What a nerve!' exploded Sam.

'Well,' I said, 'looks like we got him. But how do we prove it?'

Even Sam hadn't an answer to that one. Deep in thought we slowly wheeled our bikes out into the yard. Then we came to a halt.

Taff had said he'd do another check at home time. He was doing. And how. Outside the bike shed stood Loopy Lloyd, our Geography master, shepherding all pupils down to the main gate. Mademoiselle was at the school door engaged on the

34

same task. And at either side of the main gate stood Taff and the Walrus, like a couple of super-efficient customs officers, checking every kid's bags as they passed through.

'Huh!' said Sam disparagingly. 'What about the side door out of school?'

Loopy heard her.

'The caretaker's there,' he announced. 'With Oscar.'

Oscar is the caretaker's Alsatian. A typical candidate for the Dangerous Dogs Act.

'Well,' I said grudgingly, 'at least they're trying. Let's go and be searched.'

'Hang on a sec!' Sam sounded excited. 'When Des or whoever nicked the trainers, he must have hidden them outside somewhere, mustn't he? Didn't you say you were all searched before leaving the studio?'

''Sright,' I said.

'So where,' said Sam, 'would he be likely to hide them? Because they'll still be there, won't they?'

'Yeah,' I said, in sudden realization. 'He'd be hoping to pick them up at home time, only—'

'Only Taff's been too smart for him,' agreed Sam. 'So where?'

Polly cleared his throat. As this usually means he's had a Great Idea, we spun round to face him.

'Spill it,' I commanded.

'The b-bins.' Polly was stammering with excitement. 'There's two litter bins behind the Arts b-block.'

'Well done, mate,' I said. 'I'll make a 'tec of you yet. Come on.'

We leaned our bikes against the wall of the shed and pelted round to behind the Arts block.

Two litter bins stood staring blankly at us. Sam peered into one, then delved amongst the rubbish with both hands.

'This is *disgusting*,' she announced. 'All wet and sticky. Can't feel any shoes though.'

Polly began to rummage around in the second bin. After a few seconds—

'Hey!' he said. 'I think I've g-got 'em.'

He dived both hands into the gunge. They emerged holding a pair of rather mucky Reebok trainers.

'Gosh!' he said. 'What a relief. I'll go and tell Taff.'

'No!' I snapped 'Put 'em back.'

Polly stared at me blankly.

'P-put 'em back? But they're mine.'

'I know,' I said. 'But we want to catch the thief, don't we? Put 'em back.'

'How'll that help?' said Polly rebelliously.

'I'm with you.' Sam spoke quickly. 'Don't you see, Polly? When Taff and the Walrus think everyone's gone, they'll come away from the gate. They can't stop long anyway. There's a staff meeting, isn't there? So, when they've gone, Des'll sneak back to pick up the loot.'

'Then we've got him,' I said.

'Gosh!' repeated Polly. 'That's brill, JB. I—'

'So put 'em back,' I hissed impatiently. 'And let's hide.'

Reluctantly, Polly slid his precious trainers back into the sea of muck. He didn't actually kiss them and tell them not to worry, but I had the feeling it was a near thing.

Then we hid behind a small building which had something vaguely to do with the central heating system and waited.

We didn't have to wait long. A silence had fallen which seemed to imply that no kids were still in the area. Then a figure emerged from round the side of the Arts block and began to creep surreptitiously towards the bins. Polly was about to dart forward. I stopped him.

'Not yet,' I breathed. 'Let's catch him with them in his hands.'

We watched in silence. I'd been right. The thief was indeed Des Davies. Without hesitation he scurried across to the bin where the trainers were hidden and dived his hands into the rubbish. They emerged holding the Reeboks. I stepped forward.

'Hi Des!' I said sociably.

Des leapt high enough for an Olympic Gold. The trainers dropped from his nerveless hands to the ground. Polly leapt out of his hiding place to rescue them.

'Mine, I think,' he said triumphantly.

Des darted a terrified glance at us and turned to run. Sam blocked his way, poised ready to deliver a karate type chop.

'Go ahead,' she invited. 'Make my day.'

This friendly invitation appeared to unnerve Des completely. We closed in.

'You,' I said sternly, 'are responsible for all this nicking, aren't you?'

'Don't tell Taff,' pleaded Des. 'He'll kill me. And

37

he'll tell Dad. And Dad'll kill me. And I'll maybe be expelled.'

'And sent to a reform school,' said Polly with satisfaction.

I said, 'Promise to return all the stuff?'

'I promise,' wailed Des. 'I promise.'

I paused, uncertain what to do next. Sneaking to teachers is regarded at Moorside as a crime even worse than murder. My name would be mud. On the other hand, if the thefts continued, I should be branded as a failure by Fatso. And as Fatso (the Moorside version of a communication satellite) had already informed the entire class that he had employed me to find the thief, my Sherlock Holmes image would be damaged beyond repair. Catch-22! My brain raced But, for once, my guardian angel must have been putting in an unusual bit of over-time, because salvation was at hand.

Behind Des's back I saw two figures approaching. One was Fatso himself. The other was Jason Lang. Obviously they were looking for Des. I raised my voice.

'So you admit you stole Fatso's Walkman?' I queried in clear, carrying tones.

Fatso and Jason did a sort of emergency stop. They froze into immobility as if auditioning for Madame Tussaud's.

'Yeah. I took it,' moaned Des.

'And you'll give it back?' I said loudly.

'Yeah. Tomorrow. I'll leave it somewhere where he'll find it. Don't tell him,' begged Des. 'He'll kill me.'

Really, I thought, the number of people queuing

up for Des's blood appeared to be growing. I opened my mouth for the next threat. It was never uttered. Fatso could contain his fury no longer.

'You rotten louse!' he yelled and leapt forward, followed by Jason.

Des spun round. Too late. Fatso flung himself straight at his victim like a Scud missile. Des went down with Fatso on top of him. And, believe me, Fatso's weight must be akin to that of your average sumo wrestler. Des kicked and clawed desperately to prevent himself being suffocated, while Jason danced round on the sidelines, landing the odd kick when an opportunity presented itself. I decided the time had come for a strategic withdrawal.

'Scarper!' I hissed to Sam and Polly.

We scarpered.

As we collected our bikes we heard a yell from behind us.

'Stop!'

It was Taff's voice. We stopped and turned cautiously to face him. He arrived in dignified haste.

'Why are you three still on the school premises?'

'I had a puncture, sir,' I lied, going into my usual sponsored grovel act.

Before Taff could reply to this bit of doublespeak Sam had butted in.

'Please, sir, there's an awful fight going on behind the Arts block. Paul and I heard the din while James was messing with his bike and we went over to see what was up. But it was really scary, sir. Wasn't it, Paul?'

Polly gulped and nodded violently.

'So we ran away,' concluded Sam. 'But someone

ought to stop them, sir. I don't *think* they were
armed, but—'

'Thank you, Samantha. You three get off home,'
Taff said hurriedly, before proceeding at a gallop
in the direction of the Arts block.

'Come on,' I said. 'Before he gets back.'

'So,' said Sam smugly, as we mounted our bikes
and rode off up the street, 'Fatso will blurt out the
whole story as an excuse for fighting and so Des'll
have to admit he's been doing the thieving and
tomorrow, Polly, you can tell Taff you found your
trainers in the litter bin behind the Arts block and
Taff'll remember *where* they were fighting and put
two and two together and he'll tell Des's oldies
and—'

'We'll all live happily ever after,' I finished as
she paused for breath.

She was right too. We heard next morning that
Taff had taken Des home in his car, reported every-
thing to his dad and recovered all the loot, including
Fatso's Walkman. Polly duly reported the recovery
of his trainers and, at morning break, I waylaid
Fatso.

'You owe me five quid,' I said.

Fatso eyed me in unfriendly fashion.

'You didn't return the Walkman. Taff did.'

'It was due to me,' I said indignantly. 'You know
it was. You heard me tackle Des.'

'That's right.' Polly came to my support.

Fatso still hesitated. A crowd of our mob began
to gather as they always do when they think a fight's
imminent. I appealed to them.

'We caught Des red-handed last night. Taff only

40

came later. We found Des with Polly's trainers. You must have heard.'

They had, of course. Jungle drums have nothing on Moorside's communication system. The crowd began to close in round Fatso.

'Pay up, Fatso,' yelled someone.

'Welsher!' came a voice from the rear of the crowd.

Fatso knew he was beaten. Reluctantly, he fished some pound coins from his pocket.

'I only got three quid on me.'

'I'll take that and an IOU,' I said grandly.

Fatso handed over the coins and, amid advice and encouragement from the crowd, scribbled an IOU on a piece of paper torn from Polly's diary.

We had just completed the transaction when the bell went for the end of break.

As we filed back into school, Polly, gloomy prophet to the last, whispered, 'You'll never get that other two quid.'

I jingled the coins in my pocket.

'Wanna bet?' I said.

3
The Mystery of the Squinting Gnome

I've always considered garden gnomes to be fairly harmless little creatures but, only a few weeks after I'd added to my reputation as the school's Sherlock, we were all in dead trouble simply because of some misbehaving gnomes.

We don't go in for garden gnomes ourselves. Mum, who's Head Gardener at our house, thinks they're too twee for words and wouldn't have one if it were given away as first prize in a raffle. Polly's family aren't gnome minded either, but Polly's Aunt Jane and Uncle Ernest are really into gnomes in a big way. They've got the things lounging about all over the garden – fishing in ponds, sitting on synthetic toadstools, or just standing around gazing into the middle distance, with thoughtful expressions. His Aunt Jane even has pet names for each of them. There's Horace and Herbert and Harry and a cross-eyed one of particularly repellent appearance called Benjamin, which Polly's aunt had only recently bought in Camcaster market. Polly and I find the whole thing pretty sick-making I can tell you.

It was, however, of some interest to us as Vigilantes when some nutter in our area began nicking gnomes from different gardens.

We first saw the report in the local paper. Polly pointed it out to me.

'Seen this, JB? Aunt Jane's getting ever so worried about it.'

I scanned the report.

'It's not really local though, is it? Owley Wood's right over the other side of Elwich.'

'The thieves are getting closer all the time,' said Polly. 'Uncle Ernest says they're working down towards this way.'

'Why doesn't he hide the gnomes in his shed then?' I asked reasonably.

'Aunt Jane says they wouldn't like it,' Polly said seriously. 'She says gnomes are only happy out in the garden.'

I snorted derisively. It sounded like the thief wasn't the only nutter around.

'Benjamin and co. will have to take their chances then,' I said callously and proceeded to dismiss the matter from my mind and concentrate on beating Polly at the computer game we were playing.

It was only two days later, however, when I collected Polly at the corner of Laurel Grove on our way to school, that he broke the news to me.

'They got him last night.'

I looked at him blankly.

'Who got who?'

'Thieves took Aunt Jane's new gnome,' amplified Polly.

'Just the one?' I said.

43

'Yeah. Just Benjamin. Aunt Jane rang Mum this morning. She's ever so upset.'

'Has she phoned the cops?'

'Yeah. But she said they didn't seem very interested. Just said they'd be round later. I was wondering—'

'What?'

'Could you take on the case, JB?'

I swerved so violently that the front wheel of my bike almost tangled with Polly's. He took avoiding action.

'What d'you expect me to do?' I said. 'There's no clues or anything. The whole thing's just wacky.'

'But—'

'No,' I said. Flatly.

I mean, you can't afford to take on something with a 99.9 per cent chance of failure, can you? Even the cops shy away from that sort of case. All the papers say so. Polly looked disappointed but he said no more.

The next day was Saturday so we did our usual weekly trek to the library in Elwich. We both read a lot and are dead keen on adventure stories and detective yarns and anything really gory and terrifying. Polly had managed to get hold of a new book by one of his favourite authors and couldn't wait to get started on it. He was, in fact, trying to read the opening pages as we ambled slowly home again. I looked at him in irritation.

'Can't you leave that book alone till you get home? You've got a week to read it.'

'Wha'?' said Polly, without lifting his eyes from the printed page.

'Can't you—? Oh, forget it!' I stalked on ahead of him in disgust.

We were at that moment in Pepper Street, a narrow thoroughfare lined with small Victorian terraced houses and dingy shops on either side. It was not a pleasant street, but it did furnish a short cut to the High Street, where I'd promised Mum I'd pick up some stuff from the cleaners for her. Some of the buildings still had the old-fashioned gratings on the pavement in front of the window, with a cellar beneath them, though few of the cellars now contained coal. I began kicking any pebbles I saw down through the gratings as I passed.

Suddenly I was interrupted in this harmless pastime by a crash and a yell from behind me. I swung round.

Polly appeared to have tripped over his shoelace which had been undone and trailing for some minutes. He was lying face downward with his nose pressed against one of the gratings. His book had flown from his grasp and was lying some way off. I bent and retrieved it. Having done so I was surprised to see that Polly was making no attempt to rise. I crossed to him.

'You OK, mate?'

There was no answer. Polly remained face down on the grating. I began to panic. I bent and grabbed him by the shoulder.

'You hurt?'

Polly slowly scrambled to his feet. His face wore a dazed expression. I started to wonder if he'd concussed himself or something.

'What's up, mate?'

45

Polly turned horrified eyes to me.

'He's d-down there!' he said slowly.

Concussed out of his tiny mind, I thought. Poor old Polly. I decided to humour him.

'Who's down there?'

'B-Benjamin. In the cellar. I saw him when I f-fell.'

It took me a second or two to remember who Benjamin was, then I said, 'He can't be!'

'L-look for yourself,' said my friend simply.

I gave him a doubtful glance, then I bent down and peered through the grating.

There was certainly a gnome in the cellar. In fact there were several. The place looked like it was a gnome refuge or something. I straightened up.

'OK. So the people who live here collect gnomes. How d'you know one's Benjamin?'

'B-because of his s-squint.' Polly's stammer was becoming more pronounced, so I knew he was het up. 'You ever s-seen another s-squinting gnome?'

I had to admit I hadn't. I bent down for another look. Polly crouched beside me.

'S-see? That one.'

He jabbed a finger through the grating at one particular effigy lying on its back staring blankly up at us. It certainly had a most pronounced squint which gave it an oddly furtive expression.

'You can just see a faint mark on the b-base too.' Polly again jabbed his finger through the grating. 'I noticed that when Aunt Jane first got him. It's B-Ben all right. I know it is.'

We scrambled to our feet. Polly looked at me.

'What shall we d-do, JB?'

I frowned. Polly's blind belief in my powers has me worried sometimes. I often feel his trust in me is a bit like a jellyfish clinging to a rock.

'Let's get away from here for starters,' I said. 'The owner may be watching us from inside the shop.'

Polly darted a hunted glance at the shop window. A grimy, tatty looking window it was too, containing all sorts of old junk that I couldn't imagine anyone ever wanting, let alone buying. The shop appeared to be temporarily empty of humans, but you can't be too careful, can you? We moved off down the street. Polly returned to his original query.

'So what shall we d-do? I gotta g-get him back. Aunt Jane looks on him as *family*.'

'Shut up!' I said. 'I want to think.'

I didn't have long to think actually. Almost immediately the loud ringing of a bicycle bell just behind us caused us to spring round like guilty conspirators.

'Hi, boys!' said Sam's voice. 'You look like you're up to something. What's cooking?'

Left to myself I'd probably have fobbed the girl off with some excuse. I mean, I've nothing against Sam and she's a good third man but, as I've said, she is inclined to be bossy and to take over as leader if you don't watch her. I didn't want her coming up with a solution to the present problem before I did. Polly, however, couldn't wait to confide the gnome saga to another willing listener. He seized her by the arm.

'We've found who's nicking gnomes!' he announced dramatically.

47

'You don't know that.' My denial sounded weak even to myself.

But Sam's face lit up like that of a lion with a tasty Christian in view.

'Lordy! Have you really? Honestly, how you two get on to everything before the cops I'll never know. Who is it?'

'Owner of that shop,' said Polly, before I could utter a word. 'See, the one with those c-candlesticks and stuff in the window. The cellar's full of gnomes. One's B-Benjamin.'

Sam looked a bit blank at this, which gave Polly an opening to regale her with the whole yarn. I waited impatiently, shifting restlessly from one foot to the other.

'So we're going in to get him back,' finished Polly blithely.

'Here, hang on a sec,' I said. 'How can we? Even if we can move that grating there's no way of getting down there without a ladder. Anyway, people in the street'd be bound to notice. We'd get arrested.'

'Not for t-taking back our own gnome,' said Polly indignantly.

'Huh!' I said. 'You try that story on a cop who doesn't like kids.'

Polly looked at me.

'So what shall we do?'

The answer to that one was I didn't know. Unfortunately Sam did. She said, 'Get in round the back, of course. Come on.'

She began to wheel her bike along the street. After a slight hesitation we followed.

'I don't see,' I said, scuttling to draw level with her, 'that going round the back'll help.'

Sam gave me a look which announced quite distinctly that she thought me no better than half-witted. She said, 'These buildings all have small walled gardens at the back. The cellar goes right through. There's another grating in the back yard.'

'How d'you know?' I said.

'Lara Patel in my class. Her oldies used to have their chippy down here. They've moved now. But I went round there to play once or twice.'

She stalked on. I continued to follow, wishing that she didn't always make me feel so inadequate. We turned left into an alleyway, then left again. After a minute or two Sam stopped.

'This is the one.'

She leaned her bike against the wall. It was a high wall with an equally high wooden gate set in it. I gave the gate a tentative push without result. Then I tried the latch with no more success.

'Must be bolted on the inside,' said Polly helpfully.

Sam gave him a look of scorn.

'Of course it's bolted. We'll have to climb the wall.'

'Climb that?' Polly looked at it in horror. 'It's miles high.'

I decided to make a bid for leadership of the enterprise before Sam took over completely.

'Piece of cake,' I said casually. 'Make a back.'

Polly looked at me doubtfully but obeyed. I climbed on to him and scrabbled my way ungrace-

49

fully to the top of the wall. Sam followed. Polly glowered up at us.

'So now what do I do?'

'Dead easy,' I said. 'I climb down and unbolt the gate.'

It wasn't as easy as I'd made it sound actually, but I managed to slither down at the cost of a few broken fingernails. I turned to help Sam, only to find her already on the ground beside me. I looked up at the windows of the house. At least there seemed to be no angry faces pressed against the glass watching us. Relieved, I moved across and unbolted the gate for Polly. His first words as he entered were predictable.

'Is this wise, JB?'

I looked at him severely.

'Do you want to rescue Benjamin?'

'Well, of c-course I do, b-but—'

'Come on then,' I said. 'And move quietly. The place may *look* empty but people could be *lurking*.'

Polly gave a terrified moan. We began to move through the tangled undergrowth of the overgrown garden towards the building. I've seen Red Indian trackers on TV Westerns do this sort of thing with no trouble at all. We weren't so successful. In fact, to my anxious ears, we sounded like a battalion of furious hamsters marching on gravel. Twigs cracked under our feet, stones hidden in the long grass clattered away as we kicked them and a couple of crows on the roof announced to a waiting world that there were marauders in the garden. We might as well have taken along an entire brass band. Sam nudged me and pointed.

50

'See? There's the grating.'

We crept up to it and peered down. A group of gnomes peered myopically back at us.

'Hey!' said Polly. 'I think that one belongs to my neighbour, Miss Hunt. See – the one fishing.'

'You sure?' I said.

'Well, no. I mean, most gnomes look a bit alike, but—'

'We only take Benjamin,' I said firmly. 'He's the one you're sure of. Then we tell the cops about the rest. Now, help me shift this grating.'

The grating was stiff, rusted and uncooperative, but the three of us managed to shove it to one side. We peered down into the cellar. Polly looked doubtful.

'It's impossible. Even if we get d-down how'd we get out again?'

That thought had already crossed my mind. Fortunately I'd also spotted the solution.

'There's a coil of rope down there. I'll jump down and throw Ben up to you. Then I'll chuck the end of the rope up. You secure it. I'll climb up. Piece of cake.'

'Gosh!' Polly looked at me in admiration. 'That's brill, JB. Megacool!'

I smirked smugly. Polly may not be too full of ideas himself, but at least he appreciates genius in others.

'Well, get on with it then.' Sam sounded impatient.

I glanced down into the cellar. It looked quite a long drop. Also the floor looked very hard. I hesitated.

51

'Want me to do it?' asked Sam.

That settled it. I gave her a look of extreme loathing and jumped.

When you watch parachutists on telly they always bend their knees and roll over when they land so they don't break an ankle. I tried to do the same thing. Unfortunately my roll upset a few gnomes, but none appeared to have broken. I scrambled to my feet and began to look for Benjamin.

Luckily he wasn't too difficult to find. As Polly had said, most gnomes don't squint. I picked up the cross-eyed, villainous looking one and held it up.

'This it?'

'That's him,' said Polly excitedly. 'That's Benjamin.'

'Right,' I said. 'Catch.'

I threw the gnome up. Polly caught him clumsily. For a minute he almost dropped him again. I held my breath, but all was well.

'Well fielded,' I said. 'Now the rope.'

I picked up the coil of rope from the corner of the cellar and attempted to throw it up into the eager hands above. It's the sort of thing you often see done in escape films. The hero never has any difficulty with it. In the next few minutes I was forcibly reminded of how different real life is from the box. That coil of rope appeared to have a life and will of its own. It kept dropping back on top of me and almost braining me. I could feel Sam's scorn like a physical force. I was also becoming increasingly panicky, expecting the door of the cellar to open at any moment. And what sort of explanation can you offer to an irate shopkeeper who finds you chucking ropes round the premises? At the sixth attempt, however, I managed to get the thing high enough for them to catch.

'Tie it round a tree or something,' I instructed.

'I'll do it,' said Polly eagerly. 'I learned about knots in the Cubs.'

They trotted out of my field of vision. I waited anxiously. Then two faces reappeared above me.

'Rope secured, Chief,' said Sam. 'Up you come.'

Praying that Polly had forgotten absolutely nothing he'd ever learned about knots, I began to climb.

My trust was not misplaced. I reached the top safely and scrambled out. Sam unknotted the rope. We coiled it up again and dropped it back into the cellar. Then we replaced the grating.

'There!' I said with satisfaction. 'With luck they'll never even miss Ben. I don't suppose they do a gnome roll call. Let's scarper before anyone spots us.'

With Polly hugging Ben under his anorak, we scuttled across to the gate.

'How're we going to rebolt it?' asked Sam.

'We're not,' I said. 'Every minute we're here is risky. Perhaps they'll just think they forgot to bolt it.'

We let ourselves out and shut the gate. Polly prepared to run. I stopped him.

'Walk, you moron. Look casual.'

It's not easy to look casual when you're clutching

53

a squinting gnome to you like a chest protector, but Polly did his best.

'Shall we go straight round to Uncle Ernest's?' he asked when we had emerged safely on to the High Street.

'I'm not sure,' I said doubtfully. 'How do we explain how we got Benjamin back? Your uncle's not the sort to approve of us nicking gnomes out of someone else's cellar, is he? Perhaps we could—'

'We needn't say anything about the cellar,' interrupted Sam impatiently. 'We'll say we saw the gnome at the back of the shop and went in and bought him because we thought he was like Benjamin. Then your auntie'll say it *is* Benjamin. And, with any luck, she'll give you a reward.'

'Gosh!' said Polly. 'Sometimes, Sam, you're a real clever clogs.'

I frowned. I hate it when Sam comes up with these brilliant ideas before I do. I hastened to regain control of the situation.

'Just what I was about to suggest,' I said crushingly. 'Right. Let's get round there right away.'

Polly once more tucked the long-suffering Benjamin under his anorak and we set off at a trot, trying to keep up with Sam, who was cycling in the gutter beside us.

About fifteen minutes later, however, when we arrived at the front door of 'Eldorado' where Polly's aunt and uncle live, there was no reply to our urgent ringing of the bell.

'They must be out,' said Polly, with the air of Sherlock Holmes putting another one over on Dr Watson.

'Better still,' I said. 'Let's just leave Benjamin in the middle of the front lawn. Then we'll scarper. Save any explanations that way.'

I looked at Sam to see if she were about to object to the changed scenario, but for once she nodded agreeably.

'Good idea. You two put him in position. I'll keep watch at the gate.'

She waltzed off down the drive. I turned to Polly.

'Come on.'

We scuttled across the lawn. Polly said, 'I think I'll put him over there by the pond. See – by the one fishing. That's where he was before.'

'OK,' I said. 'But hurry.'

Polly manhandled Benjamin from under his anorak. He'd just manoeuvred him into position when we heard Sam's voice.

'Pssst!'

We swung round. Sam was racing up the drive toward us. She said urgently, 'There's a man in the street. He's got a bin bag. He's just nicked a gnome from next door but two. Hide!'

She darted into the shrubbery and crouched down. Polly was standing rigid, wearing his boiled codfish look. I grabbed him and hustled him into the shrubbery, shoving him down beside Sam. We peered out cautiously.

The man had halted at the gate. He was gazing into the garden. Suddenly his eye fell on the gnomes. He gave a quick, surreptitious glance round, then moved towards them at a crouching run. Polly clutched my arm.

'We gotta stop him.'

I nodded and fished in my pocket for my catapult. Then I picked up a small stone from the ground by me.

'That won't stop him,' hissed Sam disparagingly.

'It did for Goliath, didn't it?' I muttered.

The man had picked up the fishing gnome. He examined the base, then returned the gnome to its place where it continued to grin aimlessly. Next moment he'd picked up Benjamin and turned him upside down. A quick examination and he prepared to stuff the hapless Ben into his plastic sack.

This proved too much for Polly. The lad doesn't usually buckle many swashes I admit, but when he does kick over the traces he kicks with all the gusto of the front row of the chorus.

'Leave Benjamin alone,' he yelled and dashed out of the bushes.

Startled, the man swung round, still holding Benjamin by the base. He aimed a kick at Polly.

'Come on,' I gasped and hurtled out of the bushes followed by Sam.

In an attempt to free Benjamin, Polly, showing unexpected determination, seized the gnome's head and tugged.

The head came off.

As it did so, a small plastic packet fell to the ground. Sam dived for it. So did the man. Sam got there first. She picked up the packet and held it aloft.

'Drugs, I bet,' she said accusingly.

As I've said before, her mind tends to run on crime.

It looked as if she were right though, because the

gnomenapper panicked. He threw the now headless body onto the grass and made a run for the gate.

'Stop him!' shrieked Sam.

I raised my catapult and took careful aim. I'm usually a whizz with the thing and this time I scored a bull's-eye.

I got the man right behind the knee. He staggered and pitched forward – just in time to be caught by Uncle Ernest, who, with Aunt Jane, was at that instant coming through the gate.

'Don't let him go,' shouted Polly. 'He nicked Benjamin.'

Polly's Uncle Ernest isn't the warlike type. Neither, usually, is his Aunt Jane. But the words 'nicked Benjamin' galvanized her into action. She began furiously to belabour the robber with her handbag. By this time we'd reached them. Uncle Ernest was still clinging on to the thief in a bemused sort of way, but more like a drowning man clasping his swimming instructor than someone making a citizen's arrest. I decided I'd better take charge of the situation.

'Ring the cops,' I ordered.

Aunt Jane, casting one horrified glance at the head of her beloved Benjamin, which Polly was still clutching, aimed one final blow at the robber.

'Murderer!' she hissed and rushed into the house to obey.

Sam looked at Uncle Ernest.

'Don't let him go,' she warned.

'I can't hold him much longer,' bleated Uncle Ernest.

'You won't have to,' said Sam. She was busy

57

unfastening the broad leather belt which the gnomenapper wore on his jeans. I saw what she was up to and, with Polly's help, wrenched the guy's arms behind his back. A minute later his wrists were firmly lashed together.

'Now lie down,' I told him. 'Face down on the drive.'

By this time the wretched thief appeared completely demoralized. He obeyed without question. When the cops arrived about ten minutes later they found us sitting comfortably on our victim, with Polly's uncle and aunt taking it in turns to tell the guy what they thought about his behaviour.

It was the following evening when Polly and I heard the rest of the Benjamin saga from Sam.

'I was right about the drugs,' she said triumphantly. 'Cannabis, it was. Dad's lot raided the joint last night just as the baddies were loading a van with the gnomes. Not all the gnomes had drugs in though. Those which had were given a special mark on the base.'

'Like I noticed on Benjamin,' said Polly.

'Yeah. Well – they were being sold all over the area. At car boot sales and markets and by street traders. People in the know gave a password and got a doctored gome. Anyone else who chanced along got an empty one.'

I stared at her.

'Are you saying Polly's Aunt Jane gave the password? *She's* not a junkie, surely?'

''Course not,' said Sam scathingly. 'No. Some doctored gnomes had got mixed in with an innocent batch being sold in Camcaster market. When the gang realized what had happened they set out to get them back.'

'And began nicking possible gnomes from people's gardens,' I said.

''Sright,' said Sam.

'So we solved another case for the cops,' said Polly triumphantly.

'Yeah,' said Sam. 'But Dad's really wild about us going into that cellar. Breaking and entering he called it.'

'You told him everything?' I said.

'Had to. You ever been interrogated by an expert? So he says I'm to steer clear of any crime in future.'

'He's just jealous,' I said. 'The cops'd never have got on to it without us. Mum says they're too busy attending community relations courses to solve any crimes. Anyway, whatever your dad says you're still going to be Third Man, aren't you? You want to be in on future cases?'

'Try to stop me!' said Sam firmly.

4
Beanz Meanz Spies?

As soon as I woke up on the first Monday morning of our Easter holiday, I had the feeling it wasn't going to be my day. To begin with, I was a bit cheesed off because, since the affair of the dope-peddling Benjamin a few weeks previously, we hadn't had so much as a sniff of an adventure. Moreover, as soon as I'd finished my breakfast and announced my intention of going round to call for Polly, my mother issued her ultimatum.

'You're going nowhere, James, until you've tidied your bedroom. At the moment it looks as if the Oxfam sorting office has been battling it out in there with a recycling plant.'

'But, Mum,' I said, 'Polly'll be waiting and—'

'Then he'll have to wait a bit longer. You're not leaving this house till I've passed that room as fit for human habitation.'

I sighed but obeyed. Arguments and protests carry no weight at all with my oldies and can, in fact, lead to the ultimate parental weapon – pocket money withdrawal.

I'd just about reduced the chaos to some sort of order when I heard the front door bell ring. I ignored it, guessing it was probably only some of Mum's WI mob come for a briefing. Honestly, my mum seems to run the local WI like an army command post. But it wasn't the WI. It was Auntie May.

Auntie May is Mum's younger sister and she's OK. She's Akela to the local Cub Scouts and she's pretty adventurous for an oldie. This year she's planned to go on an abseiling course for her summer holidays. Also she drives a snazzy sports car and rides a powerful Honda motorbike and a lot of with it things like that. So when Mum called upstairs to tell me Auntie May had arrived I slid down the banisters quite eager to see her.

'Hello, James,' she greeted me. 'I've got to go into Camcaster for the day. Would you and your friends like a lift in?'

'Triff!' I said. 'All day?'

'Yes. I'm going in on business, but I'll drop you off near the town centre and collect you again at five o'clock. That OK?'

'Great. I don't know about Polly. His mum—'

'I'll ring Mrs Perkins while you get ready. I'm sure I can persuade her. What about Samantha?'

'What about her?' I said.

'She'd probably like to come too, wouldn't she? Nip round and ask her.'

'OK,' I said resignedly. 'But bags me the front seat in the car.'

Sam, who came to the door in answer to my knock, assured me that a) she'd love to come, b) that her mum, who was spring-cleaning, would be only too pleased to get rid of her for the day and c) she'd be ready in five minutes. I returned home with the glad tidings.

'Have you finished tidying your room?' Mum

61

sounded a warning note as I shot off upstairs to get ready.

'Sure thing,' I shouted back, giving a quick glance round and kicking a few stray comics under the bed. 'Come and check if you want.'

My room having passed its MOT, I charged downstairs again to Auntie May who was just putting the phone down. She grinned at me.

'Paul's on his way. I think I finally convinced his mum I wasn't hoping to hold him to ransom. Also, he's got permission to come home to tea with you afterwards.'

A few minutes later Polly, panting with exertion after running all the way, arrived. I noticed that even though it was a super-gorgeous morning and reasonably warm for early April, he was wearing his woolly cap and scarf. He hastily stuffed them into his anorak pocket when he saw my expression. I didn't comment though. I know what his mum's like.

Sam was waiting for us at the gate. We all packed into the fab sports car and Auntie May drove off, treating her vehicle as if it were jet-propelled. She said, 'What are you all going to do with yourselves over the holiday?'

'Nothing much,' I said. 'Take Polly's dog for walkies, watch telly. Nothing exciting.'

'Did you see that spy thing on telly last night?' broke in Polly. 'Dead good it was.'

'You mean when the baddie stole the microfilm from the Foreign Office and passed it to the enemy hidden in an empty can of baked beans?' I said.

'Yeah. Brill, wasn't it? I chewed my fingernails right off. Did you see it, Sam?'

Sam nodded.

'I thought it was great. I wish we could be involved in something like that. But, of course, that was London. You don't get spies and such round here.'

'Don't you believe it.' Auntie May, who had been listening to our conversation, suddenly decided to join in. 'There are foreign spies all over the place these days. Not in sleepy little Elwich perhaps, but certainly in a town the size of Camcaster.'

We all stared at her.

'Whatever would they be doing in Camcaster?' I said.

'There's the armaments factory on the Lemster Road, isn't there? Then there's the computer firm where your father works, James. Some of their stuff's in the top secret category. And what about that new place outside the town at Crawford's Mill? No one seems sure what goes on there.'

'That's true,' broke in Sam. 'Dad says it's pretty hush-hush. Something to do with communication and satellites and things he said.'

'There you are then,' said Auntie May triumphantly. 'Plenty there for any foreign power to want to get its hands on. I saw that film last night too. And I didn't think it was at all far-fetched.'

It was at that moment that I realized that Auntie May was definitely One Of Us.

We arrived at Camcaster in record time. There wasn't much traffic on the road and what there was we passed. Auntie May dropped us off near the town square.

'Be back here by five sharp,' she instructed. 'If I have to wait around I'll annihilate the lot of you.'

'We'll be there,' I promised. Auntie May gave us a quick wave and shot off. I looked at the others.

'Well, where shall we start?'

'McDonald's?' suggested Polly. 'I'm starving.'

'Could we go to Boots first?' asked Sam. 'Mum and I left a film to be developed when we were in the other day. I promised I'd see if it was ready.'

'OK,' I said agreeably. 'Boots first, then McDonald's for a nosh-up.'

We trotted off.

The film was ready and, as soon as we'd emerged from the shop, Sam was fishing the pics out of their folder to study them. They weren't madly exciting, being mostly of the Spencers' back garden with all the daffodils out. The remainder, which Sam said she'd taken herself, were of her ginger cat, Jasper, in various feline poses. We had Jasper lurking among the daffodils, Jasper sitting on the wall washing, Jasper tucking in to his din, Jasper rolling over on the lawn, Jasper indulging in a catnap and several other Jasper masterpieces.

'Aren't they terrific?' enthused Sam.

'Uh-huh,' I said noncommittally. 'Come on. Race you to McDonald's.'

We charged off down the street.

Lunch was scrummy-yummy – Big Macs and chips and loads of chocolate milk shake. Polly, whose mum's one of these health food fanatics, gobbled everything eagerly, assuring us it was the first

64

decent meal he'd had for weeks. At last, replete, we all sat back.

'What now?' said Sam.

As the visit to McDonald's had been the main aim of Polly's day, he had no further suggestions to offer. I said, 'Let's go to the park. In that film last night the spies always met in parks. They often seem to, don't they? So you never know. We might get lucky and see something suspicious.'

'We've not had a case for ages,' said Sam sadly.

'OK,' agreed Polly. 'But if we *do* meet any spies or crooks or other baddies I'm not getting involved in anything dangerous. I'm too full to run away.'

Actually the park, when we got there, didn't seem to hold out any promise of wild excitement. There were a few kids playing football, a few younger kids feeding the ducks and some women pushing prams around in an aimless sort of way. But there was absolutely nothing that looked at all suspicious and absolutely no one who looked like a spy.

We ambled along chatting desultorily, still mainly on the theme of the previous evening's film. Sam said dreamily, 'You know how that empty can with the film in it was just left under a park seat? D'you suppose they'd really do something like that? In real life I mean?'

'Auntie May said it wasn't far-fetched,' I said.

'But d'you suppose she'd know?' said Sam. 'I mean, she's never been a secret agent, has she?'

'I don't *think* so,' I said cautiously. 'Though you can never tell with Auntie May. She—'

Polly suddenly gave a stifled squeak and stopped

65

in his tracks so suddenly we almost fell over him. I looked at him in surprise.

'What's up?'

Polly pointed across the path to a seat ahead of us.

'Look!'

We looked.

'It's just a seat,' I said irritably. 'There are lots of them. What—'

'Under the s-seat,' said Polly urgently.

Sam and I followed the direction of his pointing finger. Under the seat lay a Heinz beans can. There was a pause.

'Someone's probably just had beans for lunch,' said Sam uncertainly.

I gave her a look of scorn.

'Cold? Straight out of the can? Yuk! Come on. Let's have a dekko.'

I darted across and grovelled under the seat. The others followed. A second or two later I rescued Exhibit A and we sat down on the seat to examine our find.

The tin had been opened, but the lid had not been fully cut away. About half an inch of it was still attached to the tin, just as it had been in the film. Carefully I prised it up.

'Let's see if it's empty.'

The tin wasn't empty. Inside was what looked like a roll of film.

'Lordy!' said Sam in awe.

'B-be careful.' Polly was getting windy I could tell. 'There c-could be spies all round us.'

I gave a quick glance round. Two toddlers played

on the grass while their mothers chatted. An old lady came slowly along the path with a white poodle on a lead. In the distance a child appeared to be deep in earnest conversation with the ducks. There was still absolutely no one who remotely resembled a spy. I fished out the film.

'What about fingerprints?' said Sam.

I scowled at her.

'What about them?'

'Yours'll be all over the tin now. And on the film.'

'Who's to know they're mine?' I snapped. 'I've not got a police record, have I? I want to see what's on this film.'

We all peered down at the film in my hands. I said, 'It's separate shots. All different negatives. There's six of them.'

I held one up to the light. We all studied it.

'Looks like maths,' said Polly brightly. 'Algebra or something.'

'A mathematical formula,' said Sam excitedly. 'Like in the film.'

'Could be,' I said. 'Let's see the rest.'

Two more of the negatives consisted of figures with X and Y and things. The other three appeared to be diagrams with measurements on. We all looked at one another.

'D'you think it is spies, JB?' asked Polly anxiously.

I nodded.

'Looks like it. What d'you say, Sam?'

'Can't be anything else, can it?' Sam seemed quite pleased about this. 'It's just like the telly film.'

'Auntie May said it wasn't far-fetched, didn't

she?' I said. I took another look at the negatives. 'These are probably atomic secrets or something. A formula for a new bomb or a secret weapon. left here by a traitor for the opposition to collect.'

'So what are we g-going to d-do?' Polly made his usual request for guidance. 'They might be c-coming to c-collect any minute. I d-don't think they'd be too pleased to see us. That man in the film g-got his throat cut, you know. Can't we just put the pics back where we found them and g-go?'

I gave him my equivalent of Paddington Bear's hard stare.

'And let the enemy get them? We can't do that.'

Polly shot a hunted glance round.

'So what are we d-doing? And c-could we decide quick and g-get out?'

I looked at Sam.

'The nick, d'you think? Or your dad?'

Sam was frowning thoughtfully. She shook her head.

'I daren't let Dad know. I promised I wouldn't get involved in anything else. He was really mad about that gnome lark.'

'The nick then?'

'They'd tell him, wouldn't they? And I'd be in dead trouble.'

'Even if you'd saved your country from disaster? Look, I'm not just leaving these for the enemy, I tell you that.' I gathered the negatives together and shoved them in the pocket of my anorak. 'I think Polly's right. We ought to scarper. We can think what to do about them later.'

'Hang on,' said Sam urgently. 'I've had an idea.'

She fiddled in her duffel bag and fished out the folder containing her snaps. 'There were six of those negatives, weren't there? I'll leave six of these in their place.'

'Won't your mum mind?'

'No. We've got the prints. I'll tell her we were looking at them and some of the negatives blew away.' Sam was carefully stowing six of her negatives into the Heinz beans can. Then she shoved the rest back into their folder. 'There. Now put the can back exactly where you got it from.'

I hesitated. I hate it when Sam forgets she's only Third Man and starts giving the orders. But, nevertheless, I saw the sense in her idea. With luck, the spy would just confirm there was a film in the tin and wait till he reached a place of safety before examining it. I knelt down and thrust the tin back into its original place, then rose to my feet.

'Come on,' I said. 'Let's scarper.'

Polly needed no second bidding.

It was as we were scuttling away from the seat that we noticed the man.

He was heading along the path towards us at a fair rate of knots and he appeared both worried and decidedly cross. In fact he looked as though he'd just thrown a five pound note into the air and it had come down as five pence. He had a roundish and, at the moment, decidedly red face and his head was turning from side to side like a radar scanner.

'Looks like he's lost his dog or something,' said Sam casually.

I gave a quick glance over my shoulder and nearly tripped over my own feet in excitement.

'Not his dog,' I said. 'Look.'

The man was grovelling about under the seat. Next second he had retrieved the Heinz beans can, given the inside a cursory examination and stuck the thing hastily into his jacket pocket. Then, after a hunted glance round to see if he'd been observed, he loped off across the grass. Polly expressed the feelings of all of us.

'Gosh!' he said.

'The foreign spy, d'you think, JB?' Sam sounded dead chuffed.

'Yeah,' I said with certainty. 'Pity you hadn't got your camera, Polly. We could have done with a pic.'

'There wouldn't have been time,' said Polly reasonably. 'Besides, you can't just point cameras at enemy agents, you know. They tend to turn nasty.'

'He's not got the films anyway,' Sam said with some satisfaction. 'Wonder what his bosses will do when they find they've got pictures of Jasper instead of secret weapons?'

'Cut his throat, I should think,' I said callously. 'They're quite ruthless, spies are. Even with their own people.'

'So what do we do now?' Polly, as usual, was looking to me for guidance.

'Nothing,' I said. 'We've foiled the plot. They've not got the plans.'

'No,' said Polly agitatedly. 'But we have. Suppose we g-get arrested as traitors or something? What are you going to d-do abut those photos?'

I considered the matter.

Sam said, 'I'm not letting on to Dad. He'd kill me if he thought I'd got involved in crime again.'

I had one of my sudden blinding flashes of inspiration.

'Tell you what,' I said, 'we'll wait a day or so, then just put them in an envelope, address it to the Foreign Office, London, and shove it in the post. How's that?'

'Fingerprints,' said Sam promptly.

I scowled at her.

'You've got fingerprints on the brain. OK. I'll do it and I'll wear gloves.'

Polly was staring at me in admiration.

'Trust you to think of something, JB. You're ace, mate. I think it's a great idea.'

I looked at Sam. She shrugged.

'It's OK, I suppose. Anything to keep me in the clear.'

'Right. That's settled then,' I said. I put my hand into my anorak pocket to check that the negatives were still safe, then I zipped the pocket firmly and grinned at my troops. 'A good afternoon's work,' I told them.

Polly had been anxiously consulting his wrist-watch. Now he said, 'Time's getting on. D'you think we ought—'

'Yeah,' I said. 'Don't want to be late. It'd mean explanations. Remember now – not a word to Auntie May.'

'I bet she'd be interested though,' said Polly.

'I know. But we couldn't trust her to keep her mouth shut, could we? Grown-ups stick together, you know. It's like – like—'

'The Mafia,' supplied Sam grimly.

'Yeah, well. And not a word to your oldies, Polly.'

'Let's swear an oath of secrecy,' said Sam dramatically.

So we swore a solemn oath and then galloped off to meet Auntie May.

We arrived at the town square at ten to five. It was a good job we did actually, as Auntie May drove up only a couple of minutes later. She looked pleased to see us.

'You're here. Good. Climb in quick. I'm not supposed to park here.'

So we scrambled in and she drove off, just thwarting a traffic warden, who was beginning to move ponderously across the square towards us.

'Well,' said Auntie May cheerfully, 'had an exciting afternoon?'

'Not really,' said Sam and I in chorus.

'Yeah. Rather,' said Polly at the same moment.

'So what did you find exciting, Paul, that the others didn't?' pursued Auntie May.

'It was McDonald's,' I said hastily, before Polly could open his mouth and stick his foot in it again. 'He loves going to McDonald's. He's not allowed food like that at home.'

'What a shame!' commiserated Auntie May. 'I like McDonald's too.'

We discussed food for the remainder of the journey. It was a bit boring – but safe.

Auntie May dropped us off at our front gate, refused my invitation to come in because she said her cat would be wanting his tea, and drove off with a screech of tyres. Sam looked at me.

'Remember. Mum's the word.'

'I know that,' I said irritably. 'I'm not a complete amateur, you know. I'll let you know when I've posted the things.'

Sam nodded and waltzed off up her drive. Polly and I went in to tea.

Mum, having told Polly she was pleased he could stay, began to question us about how we'd spent the day, so Polly told her all about McDonald's and I waffled on about feeding the ducks and playing in the park. She seemed satisfied – you can usually fool the oldies if you set your mind to it – and sent us off upstairs to tidy up before tea.

By the time we got down again, Dad had arrived home from work so we were all able to sit down together. Dad isn't usually very chatty at meal times. He prefers to devote his energies to the serious business of eating. Tonight, however, he obviously had news to impart.

'Funny thing happened today,' he began, as soon as the steak and kidney pie had been served out. 'We've got a new bloke working at our place. Hugo Lane his name is. He and his wife have bought one of those Georgian terraced houses overlooking the park in Camcaster.'

'Nice,' said Mum. 'I wouldn't mind one of those myself.'

'Too busy, Camcaster.' Dad dismissed the idea briefly. 'Anyway, they've got two kids. Twins. Believe me, we've heard quite a lot about Jeremy and Gemma in the short time old Hugo's been with us.'

'Proud of them, is he?' asked Mum.

My father gave a hollow laugh.

'Proud? Terrified, more like. Two real little devils by all accounts. Get up to more idiotic pranks than our James here.'

'Hey! Steady on!' I said reproachfully. I was ignored. My father was continuing.

'Today the little brutes have *really* excelled themselves. Hugo wanted to do some work on a new project last night. So he took some photos home with him – negatives to use on his viewer. Of course he meant to bring them back this morning, but he came to work in a rush and left them lying on his desk. So he dashed home in his lunch hour to get them. And what d'you think had happened?'

By this time I was beginning to have a nasty, wriggly suspicion of what might have happened. I shot a glance at Polly. He obviously hadn't twigged. He was tucking happily into the steak and kidney pie without a care in the world.

'Those negatives had vanished,' said Dad impressively. 'Disappeared into thin air. Well, of course to begin with he thought perhaps he hadn't left them on the desk after all, so he searched his study. No sign. Then he asked his wife if she'd moved them, but she swore she hadn't. It was only at that point that he thought of asking the twins. And d'you know what those infernal kids had done?'

Mum hastily assured him she had no idea.

'They'd put the negatives into an empty tin of Heinz beans they'd got from the dustbin,' my father said in disgust. 'And then they'd left the tin under a seat in the park.'

Polly, suddenly alive to the situation, choked on

a large mouthful of pie. Mum leapt up to offer first aid. My father waited impatiently for the coughing to subside before continuing his tale.

'Apparently,' he said, 'they'd got the idea from that stupid TV film last night. Television does influence children, you know. I often think James watches too much.' He broke off suddenly. 'Are you all right, Paul? You look a bit odd.'

Polly was sitting with his knife and fork clutched in a sort of defensive position, his mouth open wide enough to be mistaken for the entrance to the Channel tunnel and his eyes fixed on me with the expression of a very wet spaniel who's been taken on too long a walkies in the rain. Fortunately, my mother decided to answer for him.

'He's just had a bit of a shock. It's nasty choking like that. Anyway, what happened, dear? Did Hugo Lane get the negatives back?'

'No, he didn't,' said my father. 'That's the really worrying part. He went galloping straight off to the park, of course. At first he thought he was in luck. There was the can, under the seat just as the terrible twins had said. So he shoved it in his pocket and rushed back to work. But when we came to look at the film – guess what we found?'

Both Polly and I could have guessed quite accurately what they'd found, but we waited for the punch line.

'The original negatives had gone.' Dad paused and looked all round the table to make sure he had the fascinated attention of his audience. He had. 'In their place were six photos of a cat. Imagine! A CAT!'

'Fancy that!' murmured my mother. 'I suppose the twins—'

'The twins swore they knew nothing about it. They'd left Daddy's film in the tin, they said. Hugo says he practically had the thumbscrews out, but they stuck to their story. So God knows where those negatives are.'

'Are they important?' asked Mum.

'Vital. And if a rival firm got their hands on them – well!' My father paused expressively. 'They're so important we're thinking of offering a reward for information.'

Mum said practically, 'Have you told the police?'

'Not yet. We're hoping somehow they'll turn up. We really don't want to bring the police in. May have to, of course.'

There was a clatter as Polly's knife dropped on the floor. He scrabbled under the table for it. I shot down ostensibly to help him.

'JB,' he whispered, 'what—'

'Leave it to me,' I breathed.

We surfaced. I'd been thinking quickly during the past few minutes and come to the conclusion that we might just get away with a partially truthful explanation. Besides, there was this suggestion of a reward. I cleared my throat.

'I think perhaps,' I said carefully, 'that I know where the negatives are.'

My father froze still, a forkful of food halfway to his mouth. Madame Tussaud's would have been proud of him.

'And how do you come to be involved in this,

76

James?' he said through clenched teeth when the power of speech had returned to him.

I took a deep breath.

'Well it was like this, see. Sam and Polly and I were in the park when we saw this empty can lying around. They're always on at us at school about litter, so we picked it up. To put in the litter bin. Only then we saw the film in it.'

'Go on,' said my father dangerously.

'Well we'd all seen that film on telly, so we thought the negatives might be important. And we didn't want the wrong people to get hold of them. So we took them out of the can and put in some negatives Sam had with her.'

'Of her cat,' said my father.

''Sright. So then we put the can back under the seat. And that's all really,' I finished weakly.

My father smiled at me with bared teeth.

'Would it be too much to ask where the original negatives are now?'

'Upstairs. In my anorak pocket. They're quite safe.'

'Get them!' ordered my father.

'Now?'

'NOW!'

Obviously the usual family rule of not rising from the table in the middle of a meal was suspended in an emergency. I shot off up to my room, leaving an unhappy Polly to field any awkward questions until I returned.

A minute or two later I was handing the negatives to Dad, who received them in stony silence and held them up to the light to examine them one by one.

Having done this he put them down on the table and rose to his feet.

'These certainly look like all the missing ones. I'd better ring Hugo.'

'Before you have your pudding?' said Mother plaintively.

Dad nodded and made an impressive exit, shutting the door behind him. This was annoying, because though we could hear his voice from the hall, we couldn't hear what he was actually saying. It seemed quite a long time before he returned. When he did, he appeared, to my relief, to have had a complete change of mood. He smiled at me in friendly fashion.

'Hugo's most relieved all the negatives are safe. He thinks you children acted very sensibly and probably prevented the things being lost for ever or falling into the hands of our competitors. He said he just wished his infernal brats had the same sense of responsibility. He's proposing to give me five pounds for each of you tomorrow.'

'Five quid *each*?' I said in disbelief.

'That's what he said. In short, James, you appear to have brought off another of your brilliant mistakes.'

'Gosh, JB!' Polly looked at me in admiration. 'You're terrific, mate.'

I sat there, smiling down modestly at my pudding, and trying to look just like a normal boy completely unspoilt by success.

Sam brought me down to earth, however, when I rang her with the good news later that evening.

'It's great about the five quid, of course,' she said.

'But I don't know why you're making it sound as if you brought off the whole thing single-handed. It was my idea to replace the negatives with those shots of Jasper. And I think—'

I put the phone down gently and went into the living room to watch telly.

5

The Highwayman's House Horror

Only about ten days after the Heinz beans affair, when we had barely had time to enjoy spending our reward money, we found ourselves risking our lives in what was to be one of our most dangerous adventures.

It was all the fault of Bugs Bunny and his rotten History project.

Bugs Bunny is our History teacher at Moorside Comprehensive. He'd acquired his nickname partly because his surname was Burrows, but mostly because of his stick-out teeth, which gave him exactly the appearance of a belligerent rabbit. Not that he was belligerent. Far from it. He was as soft and wet as my bath sponge and we spent most of our History lessons running riot. To keep any sort of order that man would have needed an entire SAS unit on stand-by. His classroom usually resembled a street in Beirut on one of the latter's less favourable days. In fact, we'd have ignored his History project completely if it hadn't been that Bonzo Barker, our headmaster, had mentioned to us that he intended to check the work himself. As Bonzo makes Attila the Hun look like a leading, paid-up member of the Samaritans, we decided we'd better work on the project with vigour and dedication.

At first the thing had sounded dead simple.

'Go into the library,' Bugs had instructed, 'and get a book on local history. Then choose one character who once lived in this area, find out all you can about him or her and then write an essay of at least two pages.'

Well, you know how it is with holiday homework, don't you? At the beginning of the Easter fortnight the task was hardly visible over the horizon. Polly and I forgot all about it until the Thursday of the second week. Then, when he and Sam and I were just on our way back from walking Polly's dog, Whisky, over Farrington's fields, he said suddenly, 'Have you decided who you're going to write about for Bugs?'

'Haven't given it a thought,' I said. 'Perhaps we'd better go into the library tomorrow.'

'It's going to take ages even to *find* someone,' grumbled Polly.

'Why don't you do a joint project on Jeff Higgins?' suggested Sam.

We both looked at her blankly.

'Who on earth's Jeff Higgins?' I said.

Sam smiled smugly.

'Don't know much about local history, do you? Jeff Higgins was a highwayman way back in the eighteenth century. He lived outside Elwich in a big house near Friary Heath. By day he was quite a respected citizen – in fact, he was even a church-warden. By night, he put on his mask and a black cloak and became a highwayman. He had a beautiful black horse called Lucifer. And there was supposed to be a secret passage leading from his house out on to the heath. Eventually he was caught and brought to trial, but a woman who was in love with him smugggled him out of prison dressed as a parson, and he escaped to France. Then he married the girl who'd helped him escape and they lived happily ever after.'

I scowled.

'You're making this up!'

'No, I'm not,' said Sam indignantly. 'Cross my heart.'

'So how d'you know all this?'

'Got it in a book at home. I'll lend it you if you like.'

'I've heard something about that,' broke in Polly. 'Friary Court was his pad, wasn't it? I've seen it marked on one of my maps.'

One of Polly's weird hobbies is poring over road maps. He knows every street and back alley in the area. If he stood on Elwich town square any Saturday in summer, he could make a fortune directing Japanese tourists. I considered the matter in hand.

'Could you find your way to this Friary Court, mate?'

'If I look it up tonight I could. No problem.'

'Right,' I said, making one of those lightning decisions for which I am famous and which always lead me into so much trouble. 'We'll ride over there tomorrow afternoon. Bring your camera. A few photos of the house'd look most impressive stuck in our History notebooks. Fill up a useful bit of space too.'

'Great idea,' said Sam. 'I'll tag along.'

I glared at her.

'Your form haven't got a History project to do.'

'I know. But it was my idea and it sounds fun. Besides you two always get into a mess without me.'

I decided to ignore this slur.

'Two o'clock tomorrow then,' I said. 'Polly, can you square things with your mum?'

'If I said it was for school work I could go into orbit,' said Polly simply.

'As long as you wore your thermal vest,' I retorted. 'OK. Sam and I'll be at your gate at two.'

Two o'clock next day found us, true to my word, ringing our bicycle bells vigorously outside Polly's house. He appeared almost immediately, looking as if he were prepared for a trek across Outer Mongolia. Round his neck was slung his camera and also his binoculars, while in his hand he carried a notebook and several folded maps. A Thermos flask was tucked under one arm. All this impedimenta he deposited in the basket of his bike before joining us at the gate.

'What you got in the Thermos?' I said.

'Vegetable soup,' said Polly. 'Mum thought we might need it if we were standing around on wet grass making notes.'

Considering the day was both sunny and reasonably mild for April, though with a strong breeze blowing, I thought it unlikely we might catch a chill, but I didn't say so. I didn't want him to start the expedition in a huff.

We mounted our bikes and rode off, watched,

I noticed, by Polly's mum from behind her net curtains.

'This place,' I said. 'Is it far?'

'A fair way,' said Polly. 'I looked it up last night. We follow the main road, then turn off to Friary Mere. The heath's about a mile and a half beyond the mere.'

'Right,' I told him. 'You lead us.'

I will say Polly's no slouch when it comes to map reading. He guided us without any hesitation to the lonely stretch of wild moorland known as Friary Heath. We dismounted for a breather. Polly pointed to a largish house which stood in a hollow at the far side of the heath.

'That's it. That's Friary Court. Shall we have the soup now?'

'I've got a Mars bar,' said Sam. 'We could divide that too.'

'Great,' I said. 'Then we'll have a closer look at the house and take some pics.'

Five minutes later we had remounted and were coasting downhill along one of the rough paths which crisscrossed the heath. Sam said, 'Does anyone live there now, d'you know?'

I shrugged.

'Dunno. Perhaps Higgins' descendants. Be terrific if we could interview one of them. I bet no one else in the class has thought of anything like this.'

We arrived at the high wall marking the limit of the grounds. Set in it was a rusty wrought iron gate, beyond which a drive led up to the house. In the drive a FOR SALE notice board swung and creaked from its post. I pointed to it.

'See that? The house is probably empty. We could p'raps get in and photograph the inside too.'

I have this thing about empty houses. I always want to explore. It's just like an addiction and even though it's led me into a lot of scrapes in the past I'm still firmly hooked.

'Best leave our bikes here,' said Sam. 'I mean, if the house isn't empty—'

'Good thinking,' I agreed. 'Prop 'em up against the wall.'

'Lock them?' asked Polly.

'Better not,' I told him. 'In case of a quick get-away, see?'

Polly began to look a bit uneasy at this statement. I hurried over to the gate before he had time to make difficulties.

The gate swung open at my touch. We edged cautiously through and looked up the drive. Polly fished out his camera and began to click away busily. I examined the house while we waited.

It was not an encouraging sight. The windows were dirty, the paintwork chipped and the whole place looked dilapidated and neglected. Moreover it had a definitely sinister air. In fact it looked as though Count Dracula might have lived there in the not too distant past. To add to our discomfort, the weather appeared to be rapidly deteriorating. The sky had become overcast and the wind, which had been pleasantly fresh when we set out, was beginning to howl as if it were trying for a part in a horror movie. I shivered involuntarily.

'Well,' said Sam impatiently, 'are we going for a closer look or not?'

85

That decided me. I was leader of this expedition and I had no intention of being ousted from the position by any bossy girl.

'Right,' I said, in my best army commander tones. 'Single file and follow me.'

I began to run lightly up the drive trying to look like an SAS commander on manoeuvres. The others followed obediently. I kept a cautious eye on the windows. There was no sign of life or movement behind the grimy glass.

Near the house I stopped and held up my hand to halt my troops.

'See that?' I hissed, pointing to a window at the side of the house. The catch appeared to be broken and the window had swung open and was blowing to and fro in the wind.

'We could get in easy,' I said longingly.

'That's t-trespass.' Polly was heading for an attack of the heebie-jeebies.

''Tisn't,' I contradicted. 'The place looks as if it's been empty for years. Come on.'

I scrambled through the aperture. Sam followed. Polly hesitated, then obviously came to the conclusion he'd be happier inside with us than outside on his own, and reluctantly joined us in the room. We looked round.

Heavy blue velvet curtains, stained and covered with dust, hung down to brush the floor at each side of the window. There was no furniture in the room, apart from a huge oaken chest set against one wall. I pointed to it.

'Look at that.' I found I was beginning to whisper. 'I wonder if the old highwayman's treasure's still in there.'

'Or his s-skeleton,' said Polly nervously.

Cautiously I raised the lid. The chest was empty, except for a huge spider which scuttled gratefully away to freedom. Really, I thought, this whole thing was becoming more like a scene from a horror movie every minute It only lacked the scary music.

'Listen!' hissed Sam suddenly.

That girl has ears like an elkhound. I glowered at her.

'I can't hear anything.'

'Voices,' said Sam. 'Somewhere at the back of the house.'

'You sure?'

Sam nodded.

'Yeah. Shall we investigate?'

'M-must we?' said Polly plaintively.

I hesitated. This house was rapidly becoming the place where I most didn't want to be. But Sam was gazing at me with her 'dare you' expression and no one (least of all a girl) was going to accuse James Bond of being chicken. I made up my mind.

'We'll just have a quick look,' I said. 'It's probably nothing. Or tramps having a kip. Or something. Anyway, don't make a sound.'

Cautiously I crept across the room and eased open the heavy door. Sam had been right. There was now a definite sound of voices coming from somewhere to the rear of the house. I crept out into the hall. Sam gripped my arm and pointed.

'Behind there.'

At the far end of the hall a door stood very slightly

ajar. The voices were coming from the room beyond it.

'Wait here,' I breathed.

I edged silently along the passage until I was by the door. I peeped round it.

There were three people in the room, two men and a woman. The woman was young, clad from top to toe in black leather and with hair like scrambled eggs. The men were older. One was short and thickset, with grey hair and a small grey beard. The other was skeleton thin, with a pale skin, hollow cheeks, red hair and freckles. The only thing he looked fit for was to be employed as a government health warning. From what I could hear of the conversation, Greybeard seemed to be in command. But it was what the three were doing that caused my eyes to open wide and my heart to start banging away like a demented drummer.

The three of them were packing what looked suspiciously like solid gold bars into large suitcases. Glued to the spot, I gaped in at the scene.

'You'll need to bring the van round to the front in a minute, Karen,' instructed Greybeard.

'OK,' said the girl. 'I'm just finishing this case.'

Suddenly the power of movement was restored to me. I shot back to my companions.

'In here. Quick!' I hissed.

We bundled into the room we'd recently left and stood listening. Sam whispered, 'What's going on, JB? Who's in there?'

'Three of them,' I breathed. 'Packing gold bars into suitcases.'

'Lordy!' Sam was obviously shaken.

'Heathrow,' said Polly suddenly.

I glanced at him irritably.

'What d'you mean, "Heathrow"?'

But Sam, as usual, had got it in one.

'The gold bullion robbery two days ago. Polly, I bet you're right.'

'Elwich is *miles* from Heathrow,' I protested.

Sam frowned at me.

'You wouldn't expect them to camp on the airport perimeter with the loot, would you?' She broke off suddenly. 'Listen!' she hissed urgently.

We heard footsteps, then the woman's voice.

'I'll fetch the van round now.'

The footsteps came closer. We froze.

It was a pity that Polly chose that moment to sneeze.

It was a good sneeze as sneezes go, though, and to be fair to the lad, he made every attempt to stifle it. But it seemed to echo round that room loudly enough to stir the ghost of the old highwayman if he happened to be around. The footsteps came to a sudden halt. Then we heard them retreat swiftly. Obviously the woman had rejoined her companions. We heard the murmur of voices.

'They're on to us!' gasped Sam.

I looked round desperately for a hiding place. My eye fell on the chest.

'In there. Hurry!'

Sam ignored me and made for the window. I raised the lid of the chest and tumbled hastily in. Polly landed on top of me, knocking the breath out of my body with a wheeze like you get from those squeaky cushions you can buy in joke shops. I lowered the lid of the chest. It went smoothly into place with a faint click. Not a moment too soon. Next second we heard heavy footsteps enter the room and a man's voice say:

'No one here. You must have imagined it.'

'I didn't.' The woman was insistent. 'Someone sneezed. And look, the window's wide open. They must have escaped that way. I wonder how much they overheard?'

'Precious little from here, I should think.' The man didn't seem unduly perturbed. 'Probably some tramp looking for a place to hole up in. Heard voices and scarpered. Anyway, we'll be gone in the next few minutes. Get the van round, there's a doll.'

'OK.' The woman still sounded doubtful, but her footsteps could be heard retreating. There was a pause, then the heavier footsteps followed.

'Can we g-get out now?' Polly's voice breathed in my ear.

'Hang on,' I muttered. 'Make sure they're out of the way first.'

We waited, listening tensely. Minutes passed. Then, from outside, we heard a car coming closer. It stopped. There came the sound of heavy footsteps from the hallway and then from outside the window, mingled with panted instructions as the three presumably loaded the gold-filled suitcases into their vehicle. Eventually a car door slammed. The engine revved up, then gradually faded into the distance. It sounded as if the villains had departed.

I gradually became aware that there didn't seem to be an awful lot of air left in the chest. More painfully, I had developed cramp in my right leg.

90

There were no sounds from the room beyond. I decided the time had come to make an exit. I shoved against the lid.

The lid didn't move. I gave it a more violent shove. It remained immovable.

'What's up?' asked Polly in an agonized whisper.

'Lid's stuck or something,' I panted. 'Give us a hand.'

Polly moaned softly but obeyed. We both pushed and shoved at that rotten lid to no effect. I began to panic.

Suddenly there was a sharp click and the lid was raised. I felt a momentary sense of relief. It evaporated at once. And my heart, which had begun to sink during our struggle with the lid, now plummeted.

We found ourselves looking up into the face of the scrambled egg woman. In her hand she held a gun. It was only a small gun, but it had a vicious sort of look about it and was quite capable, I felt sure, of delivering two quick shots straight through the heart.

'I knew there was someone here,' she grated, in a voice that sounded like the vocal equivalent of Domestos. 'Good job I stayed behind to do a final clear up, wasn't it?'

Personally, I thought it seemed a pity. I tried my placating little smile routine.

'We're just going,' I said.

The woman laughed. It wasn't a nice laugh. In fact it rather resembled a lawn mower hitting gravel.

'The only place you're going is the cellar. Out of there. Quick!'

Obediently we scrambled out of the chest. The woman waved the gun at us in a threatening sort of way.

'Move it.'

We began to cross to the door. Polly wasn't quick enough and got prodded with the gun for his pains. There was no sign of Sam.

'To your right,' the woman directed. We obeyed.

There was a door at the end of the passage. Still holding the gun firmly in one hand, the woman produced a key from the pocket of her black leather jacket, unlocked the door and flung it open. Beyond the door a flight of stone steps led downwards. The woman gestured briefly with the gun.

'Down there.'

Beside me I heard Polly give a panic-stricken gulp. I hesitated, trying desperately to think of some way out. My brain seemed to be operating only on deaf-aid batteries.

'Geronimo!' yelled a voice.

Startled, we all swung round. A small figure appeared apparently from nowhere. Sam! She leapt on the woman, seizing her wrist in a judo grip and forcing her to drop the gun. I dived for it as the woman grappled with Sam. The cellar key dropped and clattered on the steps. Polly hastily retrieved it. I jabbed the gun in the woman's ribs.

'Reach for the sky!' I ordered, trying to sound like the hero of countless Westerns. It was annoying that my voice emerged as a strangled squeak.

To my surprise, however, the woman obeyed. I

stood pointing the gun at her and wondering vaguely what to do next.

Sam had no such doubts. With both hands she gave the woman one swift, sharp shove. With a yell, Scrambled Egg lost her balance and hurtled down the cellar steps.

'Come on!' shrieked Sam.

We bundled through the door. Sam grabbed the key from Polly and turned it firmly in the lock. We stood there panting.

At this point Polly uttered the most sensible remark he'd made for the whole of that rotten afternoon.

'Let's g-get out of here,' he said.

I nodded, shoved the gun into my pocket and led the way. We scrambled through the window and scurried down the drive like terrified gerbils to where our bikes waited outside the gate. Without speaking, we mounted and rode full tilt towards the heath. Nor did we pause till we were well away from that house and the lonely heath and back on the busy main road into Elwich. Here I came to a halt and the others followed suit. I looked at them questioningly.

'Straight to the nick, d'you think?'

'Yeah,' said Sam. 'I mean — we've plenty of evidence. You've got the gun. I got the number of their van. And—'

I looked at her.

'How d'you get the number?'

'I was hiding behind the curtains when they loaded the van. Come on. No time to waste.'

'Right!' I said. 'Off we go.'

At the nick we chained our bikes to the railings – you can't even trust cops these days, can you? – and made our way inside. A bored looking sergeant appeared behind one of those little windows they have and eyed us dispassionately.

'Yes?' he said, without apparent interest.

'We,' I told him impressively, 'have come to report the whereabouts of the gold bullion stolen from Heathrow. The thieves were holed up at Friary Court. Two escaped in a van with the loot. You'll find the third one locked in the cellar.'

'Oh, will we?' snorted the sergeant. 'And just who are you, lad?'

'James Bond,' I said. 'And I—'

'I'll give you James Bond,' roared the sergeant, who seemed to operate on a very short fuse. 'I'll—'

Polly came suddenly to life. He hissed, 'Show him the gun, JB.'

'What? Oh. Yeah.' I fished the gun clumsily from my anorak pocket and brandished it at the sergeant.

The sight of the weapon apparently concentrated the cop's mind wonderfully. In no time at all we were escorted to another room, where we told our story all over again to a grey haired man with a face like a despondent bloodhound and eyes which reminded me of loaded pistols.

Finally Sam produced the bit of paper on which she'd scribbled the van's number.

'It was white,' she told him. 'Very dirty. A Bedford, I think.'

'Right.' The Bloodhound made a note. 'I'll get a call out. And the woman's in the cellar, you said?'

'Yeah,' I said. 'We made a citizen's arrest.'

'I see.' The Bloodhound eyed us curiously. 'One thing. What were you doing in the house at all?'

Polly, obviously seeing a prison cell looming ahead, swallowed convulsively. I said, 'It was a History project, see? Famous people who once lived around Elwich. Friary Court once belonged to a highwayman.'

'Your teacher should have known better than to encourage you to go into empty houses,' said the Bloodhound severely.

'We won't do it again, sir,' I assured him, swiftly going into my well-practised sponsored grovel.

'See you don't. You were in considerable danger. In fact, you were lucky to come out of it unharmed.'

We all nodded earnestly, trying to look like honest, upright citizens. It seemed to work. We were thanked for our help and politely dismissed while the cops got on with the mopping up operation.

After this we rode home and all got into trouble because we were late for tea. I tried to explain to my oldies that we'd caught the Heathrow bullion thieves, but, as usual, I wasn't believed and Dad bawled me out for telling lies and making silly excuses. Sam was luckier, because her dad rang the nick for corroboration and got it, but he wasn't very pleased about her going into the empty house. He came round later in the evening, with Sam in tow, to tell us the cops had collected the scrambled egg woman from the cellar, but the van still hadn't been located. After this, of course, my oldies had to believe my story. Did they apologize? Not a bit of it.

Just bawled me out again for trespassing in empty houses.

You can't win with grown-ups, can you?

Next morning though, I heard on the radio at eight o'clock that the bullion thieves had been caught driving through Liverpool with the loot. Probably, said the newsreader, they were attempting to leave the country.

I paused in the snap-crackle-popping of my Rice Krispies to give the oldies my own favourite version of Paddington Bear's hard stare, as I waited for some word of congratulation. I didn't get it. Dad continued to read the paper. Mum said, 'I will say, our police are pretty efficient. They usually get their man, don't they?'

'With a little help from others,' I said sourly.

6

The Invisible Clue

After our terrifying ordeal in the highwayman's house our lives proved dead boring for the next week or two. However, as we were in the middle of exams at school, this was perhaps a good thing. And I have to admit, here and now, that our next case could not be classed among my more successful efforts. In fact, it began badly and then steadily deteriorated and it was only by the greatest good luck that I emerged from it with my reputation as a sleuth still intact.

It began quite simply with a phone call one evening as the oldies and I were watching telly.

'Get that, James, will you?' said my dad, without taking his eyes from the screen.

I sighed but obeyed, hoping that Miss Marple wouldn't have solved the case before I got back. I was lucky. The voice at the other end of the line said merely, 'Is Mr Bond in?'

'Yeah,' I said. 'I'll get him,' and bolted back into the living room with the glad tidings. My father frowned.

'Did he say who it was?'

'Nope,' I said, gazing at the screen.

'Did you ask him?'

'Nope,' I said briefly.

My father muttered something fierce but indistinguishable and departed to the hall. It was quite a time before he returned. In fact, Miss Marple had solved the crime, the criminal had committed suicide and everyone else was living happily ever after by the time he re-entered. As Mum switched off the telly she said, 'Who was it, dear?'

My dad decided to answer that question with another.

'D'you remember Peter Maitland?'

Mum looked thoughtful.

'Vaguely. Used to work with you, didn't he? Then he got a better job somewhere else and left?'

'That's the blighter.' My father sounded pretty unchuffed about it. 'Left about five years ago and we lost touch. Anyway, it seems he's going to be in Camcaster for a week or so. Some inspection job connected with that new hush-hush place at Crawford's Mill. He works at their head office now. He was rather cagey about what he was actually doing.'

'So why ring you?' asked Mum practically.

'Wanted to know if we could put him up for a few nights,' said my father cautiously. 'He said he'd been ringing round the hotels in Camcaster and they were all full.'

'And you said?' Mum's voice sounded a dangerous note.

'I said he could have our Sue's room if it was only for a few nights,' said Dad. He saw the expression on Mum's face and finished weakly. 'I didn't think you'd mind.'

'You might have asked me,' Mum snapped. 'When's he arriving?'

'Well, tomorrow actually. Fivish, he said.' My

98

father gave Mum the apologetic, smarmy type of smile I tend to use myself in times of trouble. Mum uttered a long-suffering sigh.

'It'll only have to be for a day or two. If Susan wants to come home for the weekend—'

'I know. I told him. He said that was OK.'

'Big of him,' said Mum tartly.

I told Polly and Sam about the expected visitor as we cycled to school next morning. Sam said, 'He's not one of those boring oldies who thinks he's good with kids and wants to tag along with us, is he?'

'Shouldn't think so,' I said. 'I think he'll be in Camcaster most of the time.'

'Is he a British agent or something?' said Polly eagerly. 'You know they're up to all sorts of things at that Crawford's Mill place. Communication satellites and such. All top secret stuff.'

'Dunno.' I brightened. 'Wouldn't it be great if he were and he was hiding out here because the baddies had put a death threat on him and—'

'Rot!' said Sam. 'He's probably just an accountant or an auditor or someone like that who's going to check the books. You two watch too much telly.'

I shrugged.

'Whatever he is, we're stuck with him for a week, so I hope he's not a "children should be seen and not heard" type.'

When I got home from school that evening I found that our visitor had already arrived and was talking to Mum in the sitting room. I eyed him cautiously as I was introduced.

I saw a man of medium height with smooth dark

99

hair, a pale skin and a soft monotonous voice. To describe him as wooden would have caused the Forestry Commission to sue for libel. He wore a dark grey suit, a white shirt and one of those ties that looks as if it's trying to tell you something about its owner being the product of some really posh school. In fact, my first impression of Mr Peter Maitland was that he was so sleek he probably left oil marks every time he got out of the bath. I disliked him on sight.

In the course of the evening I saw nothing to make me change my opinion. My dad had said he hadn't been in touch with the guy for five years. After five minutes I could see why. His conversation was dead boring, particularly conducted as it was in a flat, unexpressive monotone. In fact, if it had been left to him to announce the outbreak of the Second World War I don't suppose anyone would have come. In addition, he appeared to have the same quick sense of humour as your average garden gnome. And he talked non-stop. For the first time in my life I went to bed without being told.

It was the same at breakfast. Mr Maitland kept up a steady monologue. He tried at first to question Dad about his work and how, as he put it, 'the old place was battling along these days'. But Dad just buried himself behind the morning paper and uttered the odd grunt in reply. I crunched noisily and determinedly through my cornflakes without paying any attention. Which, of course, left Mum as sole representative of the Bonds to keep the conversational ball rolling. She coped very well, but I could tell she wasn't pleased.

The situation didn't improve over the next few days either. In the end, I took the coward's way out and spent as much of my spare time as possible either at Polly's pad or round next door at the Spencers'. And it was this that led, indirectly, to all the trouble.

I'd gone round to Polly's earlier than usual because it was Friday so I had no homework to bother about. He opened the door to me himself and I could tell at once that he was excited about something. He said, 'Gosh! I'm glad you're early, JB. Come on up. I've got something that'll interest you no end.'

As I followed him upstairs to his luxurious bed-sit, which turns me green with envy whenever I visit him, I said, 'Got a new computer game for me to beat you at, then?'

Polly shook his head.

'Nothing like that. Wait till you see.'

Once we were happily settled on the floor of his pad, he handed me a sheet of paper.

'Can you read what's on that?'

I gazed down at the paper in my hand. It was completely blank. I turned it over. The other side, too, was a white expanse of nothing. My expression was equally blank as I gazed at Polly.

'What d'you mean – read it? It's blank, you thicko.'

'It's not. Watch.'

Polly snatched the piece of paper from me, produced a fattish sort of felt pen from a small, green packet and began to rub it over the blank sheet. Wondering vaguely if the lad had lost his marbles

I stared at the paper. Then I did a double take. Words were appearing on the white sheet. They were brownish and very faint, but, as I watched, they gradually darkened until they became legible. In block letters I read:

BET THIS SHOOK YOU.

'Cor!' I said. 'Magic. How d'you do that?'

Polly, looking triumphant, laid the paper on the floor between us.

'Invisible ink,' he said proudly. 'I bought the pack at the joke shop. What you write's quite invisible till you use the developer. Then it shows up. Like developing a photo in a way.'

'Triff!' I said. 'Let's have a go.'

Polly handed me what looked like an ordinary, cheap ballpoint pen and a clean sheet of paper. I eyed it doubtfully.

'This all I need?'

'Sure,' said Polly. 'Go ahead.'

After a moment's thought, I scrawled a few words on the paper.

'OK,' I said. 'How long do I wait before I develop it?'

'Only a second or two. Let it dry. Now try it.'

Eagerly I rubbed the developer over the paper. The words JB IS A BRITISH SECRET AGENT appeared before my eyes as if by magic.

'Great!' I said. 'We could write messages to each other in class, couldn't we? The teachers'd feel real charlies when they confiscated them and found blank paper. Then we could use the developer and – bingo!'

The rest of the evening was spent with us pretending to be spies and passing messages to each other until Polly's mum yelled up the stairs to say it was nine o'clock and shouldn't I be going home?

We told Sam all about the invisible ink next morning when we encountered her in Elwich on our usual Saturday morning jaunt to the library. She was pretty impressed I could tell.

'It could come in quite useful, that could,' she said judicially. 'I mean, suppose one of us was kidnapped or something? We could send a message like that without the baddies ever realizing what we were up to. It was bright of you to suss it out, Polly. I think we should each get some.'

We all finished up going to the joke shop for both Sam and me to spend some of our meagre pocket money on a packet containing pen and developer, plus some ideas for codes and ciphers. A complete spy kit, in fact.

On Monday I gave in my French homework to Mademoiselle with 'Mademoiselle est une imbécile' written beneath it in invisible ink. When it was returned to me next day with the mark nine out of ten and the comment, 'Très bien, James' written across it, Polly and I fell about laughing. When we told Sam, however, she merely raised her eyebrows and said coldly, 'We bought this equipment to use in an emergency, you know. Not to waste it being stupid.'

Honestly, sometimes she sounds just like our deputy head, Mrs Wallis, who's the mother of all battle-axes.

Amid all this fun and games, however, the shadow of Mr Peter Maitland hung over me. He

103

was still very much with us and still talking. I even began to pray for Susan to ring up announcing that she was coming home for the weekend and would require her room. I also began to wonder if there was any way I could personally hasten his departure. It was obvious that my oldies were as browned off with the guy as I was, but grown-ups seem to think they've got to be more polite and tactful than we'd consider necessary.

I mentioned the problem to Polly and Sam as we rode home from school next day.

'There must be *something* we could do,' I said desperately. 'He's driving us all bonkers at home.'

Sam drew into the kerb and dismounted.

'Let's have a council of war,' she said briefly.

I gave her a warning frown. Once more Sam was forgetting that she was merely Third Man not Chief. However, Polly had already dismounted, so I braked and stood straddling my bike in the gutter, which at least gave me the more commanding position. Sam said thoughtfully, 'My dad always says that if you dropped a note through everyone's letterbox one night saying, "ALL IS DISCOVERED. FLY!" the town'd be more than half-empty next morning.'

I shrugged.

'Shouldn't think he's got anything to be discovered. He's just a wimp.'

'Perhaps,' said Polly, 'you could search his room. After all, he's in the same house.'

'Search his room?' I said blankly. 'Why?'

'To see if he has any guilty secrets. I mean, in

104

those Agatha Christie films on telly the murderer's always the most unlikely one of the lot, isn't he?'

I glowered at him.

'You're not suggesting we've got a murderer in the house, are you?'

'Well, no, but—'

'Polly's right though,' broke in Sam. 'You never know what you might find. And it would be the most terrific lark. I'd do it like a shot if he was at our house.'

About to make a scathing reply, I hesitated. As usual, the irritating girl was right. It would be the most terrific lark. I had a sudden vision of myself, torch in hand, creeping round his room and finding something really incriminating. A gun perhaps, hidden amongst his socks, or even a cache of stolen jewels. Before I knew it, I was hooked.

'Not a bad idea really,' I said slowly. 'I may try that. Tell you what, I'll do both. I'll write the "ALL IS DISCOVERED" note and leave it on his dressing table with the gun on top of it. That'll shake him.'

Sam looked at me blankly.

'What gun?'

'The gun I find hidden in his room, of course. Well, I mean, it may not be a gun, but—'

'I bet there'll be something,' Polly said eagerly. 'Trust you, JB. You've got a nose for this sort of thing. You'll suss him out.'

'Do my best,' I said modestly.

'Tonight?' said Sam.

I stared at her.

'What d'you mean – tonight?'

105

'Are you going to search his room tonight?'

That brought me up pretty sharpish I can tell you. It's one thing to make these plans in front of an admiring audience. It's quite another to put said plans into operation on your own. The other two were gazing at me eagerly. All right for them, I thought bitterly. They weren't the ones taking all the risks.

'I don't know about tonight,' I said cautiously. 'I've got to find the right moment. I can't search his room while he's in it, can I?'

'Chicken!' jeered Sam.

I reddened.

'I'm not. It's OK for you. I'm the one facing the flak. So I make the decisions. Right?'

Sam relented.

'Fair enough. Anyway, let's make it a team effort. I'll write the note. Polly can provide the pen and paper. Then, if the plan fails and there's a row, we'll all be in it together. Give us a sheet of paper, Polly.'

Obediently, Polly fished in his briefcase, tore a sheet from an exercise book and handed it to Sam.

'And a pen,' she said impatiently.

Polly produced a Biro and handed it over. Then he said, 'Gosh! I almost forgot. I did zillions of messages for each of you last night in that invisible ink. Really spooky. Here you are.'

He dug out several apparently blank sheets of paper from his briefcase and gave a couple to me and two more to Sam.

'Ta.' I stuffed the papers into my pocket. 'I'll develop 'em later.'

'They're dead good,' said Polly enthusiastically. 'I spent ages doing them.'

'Is mine the same?' asked Sam.

Polly shook his head.

'No. But they sort of link up. You need to compare notes with JB in order to make sense of it. Real spy stuff.'

'Sounds great.' Sam tucked the papers away in her saddlebag. 'Here, JB. This OK?'

She passed me the lined sheet on which she'd printed in block letters:

THE GAME'S UP. ESCAPE NOW.

I looked at it doubtfully.

'You've altered the words.'

'I know. This sounds more with it. What d'you think?'

'It'll do.' I folded the paper and shoved it in my pocket. 'Come on. I want my tea.'

We remounted and cycled off.

The matter wasn't referred to again until we'd arrived home. As Sam wheeled her bike into their drive she said, 'Let us know in the morning how you went on.'

I stared at her. Blankly.

'You are doing the search tonight, aren't you?' she hissed.

'I'll see,' I said desperately. 'If there's a chance I'll take it.'

I made my escape indoors, half of me feeling quite bold and adventurous and the other half hoping there wouldn't be a chance. A state registered coward, that's me.

I stowed my bike in the garage and galloped into the kitchen. Mum looked up.

'Oh James, I just want to slip next door with this book I promised to lend Samantha's mother. I've left you a snack to keep you going till teatime.'

'Fine,' I said, my heart suddenly beginning to beat at twice its normal rate as I realized this was IT. Next moment Mum had waltzed out through the back door and I was alone.

It was no good stopping to think about it. If I did, my courage (what little there was) would probably fail me altogether. And anyway, there just wasn't time. I shot upstairs and opened the door of Susan's bedroom.

I will say, the place was a lot more orderly than when Sue was in possession. With my heart pounding so loudly it could probably be heard by my mum next door, I began my search.

To my disappointment, there were no guns hidden among Mr Maitland's socks, or secret radio transmitters on the wardrobe shelf. In fact there was nothing in that rotten room that couldn't have been found in the bedroom of any innocent, law-abiding citizen. I even stood on a chair to peer over the top of the wardrobe. Nothing. Short of rolling back the carpet and removing the floor boards, there seemed little else I could do.

After a moment's hesitation I decided to leave the threatening message anyway. If it didn't work (and I could see no reason why it should) I could always pretend it was a daft joke and intended for Susan next time she returned home.

I delved into my pocket and fished out several

sheets of paper. The top two were blank. I gazed at them, frowning. Then I remembered. Polly's secret messages. The third sheet, with Sam's careful printing on it, was the one I wanted. I opened one of the drawers in the dressing table and laid the note on top of Mr Maitland's clean shirt, before carefully closing the drawer again.

It was just as I was going to retrieve Polly's invisible messages from the bed where I'd left them that I saw the suitcase.

It was sticking out slightly from under the bed and I suddenly remembered that, in a similar situation, 007 had found incriminating evidence in the baddie's suitcase. I eyed the case thoughtfully. My better nature told me I shouldn't open it. My better nature lost. I lifted the suitcase on to the bed and tried the catches. They sprang open at my touch. I raised the lid.

The suitcase was empty except for a large manilla envelope.

This is it! I thought triumphantly. I picked up the envelope, carefully raised the flap and slid out one or two sheets of thin paper. Full of the thrill of the chase, I was about to unfold them when I heard the back door open and my mother shout, 'James. I'm back. Where are you?'

In panic I dropped the papers on the bed, but worse was to come. I heard Mum continuing, 'Hello, Peter. I didn't realize you were following me in. You're early, aren't you?'

I heard Mr Maitland reply, but by this time I was too unnerved to distinguish the words. I scrabbled desperately for the papers, stuffed them back in their envelope, returned the envelope to the suitcase and shoved the case back under the bed all in one swift panic-stricken movement. Next moment I heard Mr Maitland's footsteps in the hall below. He was going to come up to his room. I shot a quick glance round to make sure I'd left no traces of the search. My eye caught Polly's invisible ink messages, still folded accusingly on the duvet. I hastily stowed them in my pocket and shot out through the door and back to my own room. Not a second too soon. I could already hear Mr Maitland on the stairs.

'James!' came my mother's voice again. 'You've not eaten your sandwich. Aren't you well?'

'Just coming,' I yelled.

I flung my anorak on the bed and shot out on to the landing, giving Mr Maitland a grovelling little smile as I passed him. Then I rushed agitatedly downstairs and into the kitchen. Mum looked at me.

'Are you all right?'

'Fine,' I lied, while my heart stopped trying to punch its way through my ribs. 'Just been checking I'd got all the books I needed for my homework. We've got a whole pile tonight.'

'That's a good lad.' My mother sounded vaguely surprised at my unaccustomed virtue. I decided to distract her mind.

'Jolly nice sandwich,' I said indistinctly through a mouthful of it.

This did the trick. I knew it would. It produced Mum's usual reflex action.

'Don't speak with your mouth full, James,' she

said automatically. I drew a deep breath of relief. I'd got away with it.

About half an hour later, when Dad had arrived home and we'd all sat down to our evening meal, Mr Maitland cleared his throat in a way that conveyed some important announcement was imminent. We all waited. He said, 'I'm afraid I shall have to leave immediately after tea. I've just been packing.'

I almost choked on a mouthful of fish pie. It had worked! I thought. Sam's wacky idea had worked. He'd read the note. He thought we knew some guilty secret of his. What a pity I'd not had time to examine those papers in the suitcase! Mr Maitland was continuing.

'I had an urgent call from Head Office this afternoon. I have to be back in London first thing in the morning. I want to thank you both for putting me up and making my stay so pleasant.'

Mum and Dad both uttered polite disclaimers. Dad was looking really chuffed, but Mum managed to conceal her joy better. She's quite a star in the local amateur dramatic society is Mum.

Anyway, as soon as the meal was over Mr Maitland, apologizing for rushing off, carried his suitcases out to his car and we all stood at the gate waving like overzealous semaphore enthusiasts till he'd driven off. Then Dad said simply, 'Thank God for that,' and I went up to my room to do my homework, still wondering if Sam's threatening message had been the cause of our visitor's abrupt departure.

It was some time later that night, when I'd eaten

my supper and was just on the point of crawling into bed, that I remembered I still hadn't so much as glanced at Polly's invisible ink messages. He was bound to ask me about them on our way to school in the morning. I opened the wardrobe and took the folded papers from my pocket.

I got the developer out of the drawer and unfolded the papers. Then I froze. Instead of the blank papers I'd expected to see, I was holding what looked like a couple of computer print outs.

For a second I gazed down at them, looking as blank as the papers should have been. Then it dawned on me. I'd heard about people going cold all over with shock. Believe me, that's no exaggeration. I turned into an ice cream soda the instant I realized that these must be the papers I'd taken from Mr Maitland's suitcase. And so he was now travelling down to London with Polly's daft messages.

I don't mind telling you I panicked and sat on the side of the bed trembling like that boring old aspen leaf. These papers were likely the poor guy's report. Worse, if he contacted Dad and asked about them, I'd be questioned. No doubt about that. If anything goes wrong in our house I'm always Suspect Number One. One of these days Dad'll blame me for the weather. Somehow I'd got to get myself off the hook. But how? I racked my brains.

Then suddenly I had one of my flashes of inspiration. I checked the plan in my mind. It seemed feasible. I listened. The oldies were still watching telly. If I was quick . . . .

Seizing the printed papers I opened my bedroom

door and listened again. All clear! I nipped silently along the landing and into Sue's room.

Once there it was the work of a moment to shove the papers under the bed. Mum would be doing out the room in the morning, in case Susan arrived unexpectedly at the weekend. With luck, she'd think Mr Maitland had accidentally dropped his papers there during his hurried packing. There'd be no reason to suspect me.

About half an hour later when Mum opened the door of my room and looked in on her way to bed, I was curled up under my duvet apparently fast asleep. In actual fact I was wide awake, with my mind racing. I was trying to think of a suitable yarn to spin Polly and Sam next morning. Something that would make me a 007 figure, not a wimp who mucked things up. After a time, the germ of an idea came into my mind. Sleep on it, I thought.

Sam was waiting at her gate when I set off for school next morning. She said, 'Any luck with the search, JB? Or the note?'

'Well, he's gone,' I said. 'Left last night. Said he'd been called away suddenly.'

Sam's face lit up as if I'd pressed a switch.

'There you are then. He's got a guilty secret. Did you find anything in his room?'

I nodded importantly.

'I did. But then I was nearly caught. It was ghoulish!'

'Lordy!' Sam looked all agog to hear the horrors. 'Do tell.'

'Hang on a sec,' I said. 'Here's Polly.'

'Hi JB!' Polly braked to a halt beside us. 'Did you do the search?'

'Yeah,' I said casually.

'And he found something,' said Sam. 'Go on, JB. What was it?'

'Papers,' I said. 'Secret plans. He's a spy all right.'

'Gosh!' said Polly. 'A real spy. And staying in your house! What did you do, JB?'

'I took the papers,' I said. 'And I put those secret message ones you gave me in their place.'

'Had you developed them?' said Polly anxiously.

I shook my head.

'No. They were still blank.'

'I tried to read my message,' interrupted Sam. 'But it didn't make sense. I thought perhaps it was in code. Was it?'

'Not really,' said Polly. 'But there were two stages to it. First of all, everything was written backwards – like SAM would be MAS, see?'

Sam frowned.

'Even then, I don't think—'

'No. Well. I told you. To get it, you had to work with JB. You only had every other word on your paper. JB had the words in between. Clever, wasn't it?'

'And after all that,' I said, 'what was the message?'

Polly reddened.

'I'd copied out pages from one of Carol Anne's old story books. It was all about Thomas the Tank Engine.'

'Never mind about that,' Sam broke in. 'That's

just a game. This is for real. JB, did he twig? Or has he gone off with the false papers?'

'Went off with them,' I said. 'Piece of cake it was.'

'It *was* pretty bright of you,' admitted Sam. 'Couldn't have done better myself.'

I smiled modestly. Sam was continuing.

'So where are the spy's papers now, JB?'

This was the tricky bit. I pursed my lips.

'I'm not at liberty to say at the moment. Come on. We're going to be late for school if we don't shift.'

I sprang on my bike and set off through the traffic before Sam could reply.

It wasn't until my father arrived home that evening that the next instalment of the Maitland saga unfolded. Almost as soon as Dad was in the hall, Mum said, 'I found some papers belonging to Peter Maitland under the bed in Sue's room this morning. It looks as if they were dropped while he was packing and he overlooked them.'

I breathed a sigh of relief. I'd done it. I was in the clear.

'I was going to post them to him,' Mum was continuing, 'then I thought it might be better if you faxed them through. Anyway, Peter rang up about lunchtime asking if I'd found some papers belonging to him. He was most relieved to know they were safe. But he said to post them to his home address not fax them to his head office.'

'Curious,' said Dad. 'Have you posted them?'

'Not yet. He said there was no desperate rush. Why?'

'Let's see them,' said Dad eagerly. 'I'd like to know what he was up to.'

Mum produced the papers from the dresser drawer. Dad scanned them closely. I watched. Apprehensively.

After a few minutes Dad let out a low whistle and looked up.

'Well?' Mum and I spoke together.

'Well,' said Dad, 'you know how cagey Peter Maitland was about his exact job? It's because he's a special investigator for the head office of that Crawford's Mill firm.'

'And?' said Mum.

'And they were suspicious that someone at the Camcaster branch was fiddling the firm's accounts. Maitland was sent down to look into it. As far as I can tell, these papers are his report. And proof there was indeed a fiddle going on.'

'So why not fax them straight through?' said Mum.

Dad tapped the papers.

'Seems there's an accomplice at head office, identity unknown. So Peter's got to make sure these papers don't fall into the wrong hands.'

'Cor!' I said. 'Real spy stuff.'

Dad sighed.

'You see spies everywhere, James. Peter Maitland is a qualified accountant, employed to investigate the accounts. That's all. Anyway, I'll write a note to enclose with these papers and post them to his home in the morning.'

I had one of my sudden flashes of inspiration.

116

'I'll post 'em if you like,' I said. 'On my way to school.'

Next morning I waited until Polly had joined Sam and me at the corner of Laurel Grove, then I waved the envelope containing Mr Maitland's report.

'Just got to shove this in the pillar box. Won't be a tick.'

I darted off, leaving Polly holding my bike. When I rejoined them I said casually, 'Well, that's the end of the Maitland case. I've just posted those papers. With my report, of course.'

'Where to?' said Sam suspiciously.

I gave her my most superior smile.

'Sorry. I can't tell you. On this one my lips are sealed. Official Secrets Act, you know. Anyway, I foiled his plot.'

'*We* foiled the plot,' said Sam coldly. 'My message telling him to escape panicked him and—'

'And I had the idea of searching his room,' added Polly.

'And I did it,' I said. 'I was the agent in the field. I took the risks.'

'You were ace, JB,' said Polly hurriedly.

I looked at Sam. I doubt if I'd really impress her if I walked barefoot across Antarctica in the dead of winter. Point was – did she believe my story? There was a pause.

'The whole thing sounds pretty wacky,' she said at last. 'But then, spy things always do on telly. So I s'pose it's true. You were brill, Chief!'

This, from Sam, practically amounted to inclusion in the New Year's Honours List. Praying

117

silently that she'd never discover the truth, I said modestly:

'Oh, it was nothing. Really.'

7

The Case of the Snoring Chimp

To our disappointment, no cases turned up for the entire length of our spring half term holiday. But we'd not been back at school for more than a week when we were once more plunged unwittingly into an adventure. And all because of a pen.

It was Sam who first found the pen. The three of us were on our way home from school and we'd just dismounted from our bikes in order to visit our favourite sweet shop when she suddenly bent down to pick something out of the gutter.

'Hey!' she said. 'See what I've found.'

She held the object out for our inspection. It was an ordinary black and silver ballpoint pen, a bit grubby from lying in the gutter, but quite an expensive looking job for all that.

'Bet someone's dropped it as they got out of a car,' I said. 'Does it write?'

'Half a tick.' Sam fished in her pocket for a bit of paper and scribbled eagerly. 'Works a treat,' she announced.

Polly eyed the pen avidly. He has this thing about pens. He collects them like other people collect pop star portraits. In school he lugs around a pencil case packed full of the things of every possible make

119

and colour. I shouldn't be at all surprised to find
he had pet names for all of them.

'D'you want it?' he asked Sam. 'Because if not
I—'

Sam gazed at him thoughtfully.

'Well – finders keepers and all that. I'd settle for
a good swap though.'

'I've got Jason Donovan's latest single,' offered
Polly.

'Done!' said Sam promptly. 'Let's collect it from
your place before you change your mind.'

So we bought our sweets and, chewing happily,
cycled round to number seven Laurel Grove where
Polly lives. Then Sam and I hovered at the gate
while Polly dashed inside and emerged a minute or
two later with the disc. The hand over completed,
Polly clipped the pen into the pocket of his school
blazer, and Sam, drooling over the picture of Jason
on the sleeve of the single, remounted her bike to
continue our journey home.

That, of course, should have been the end of the
matter. Only it wasn't.

It was just after eight o'clock when Polly rang
me. He sounded oddly excited.

'JB – could you come round for half an hour?
Have you finished your homework?'

'Just about,' I said. 'I was going to watch the
thriller on telly. What's up?'

'I don't want to talk on the phone,' said Polly
mysteriously. 'But I – it's this pen – there's something a bit odd.'

I was intrigued. Was the innocent looking ballpoint really a disguised dagger or a blowpipe cap-

able of firing poisoned darts at an enemy? Not far-
fetched for these days if you believe all the media
horror stories. I said, 'OK. I'll tell my oldies you're
stuck on your French and want me to give you a
hand. With you in ten minutes.'

It was, in fact, less than ten minutes later that I
was hammering on Polly's front door. He opened it
himself, which was a relief as I'd imagined having
to face the usual unfriendly interrogation from his
mum.

'What's all this about?' I queried.

'Ssh!' Polly put his finger to his lips in melodram-
atic fashion. 'Top secret, JB. Come up to my pad.'

As I've said before, Polly's luxurious bed-sit has
everything – portable telly, computer, music deck,
the lot. With the amount of gear he's got he could
run his own space station. Agog with curiosity, I
followed him up there.

On the top of his desk stood his FM radio. Polly
pointed to it.

'See that?'

'Of course I can see it,' I said irritably. 'Seen it
many a time. Not managed to tune in to an alien
space ship or something, have you?'

Polly loves messing about with radios or, in fact,
any electronic equipment. He's quite a whizz kid at
it too. When he grows up he'll probably be recruited
by MI5 for some of their dirtier surveillance jobs.
He gave me a look of reproach.

'I was trying,' he said with dignity, 'to pick up
the police news. You can, you know. Hear what
they're telling the guys in the radio cars. It's dead

121

interesting sometimes. Only tonight – well – I got something else.'

'Get on with it,' I said. 'The suspense is killing me.'

'OK. Listen.' Polly switched on the radio. Next second I heard his mother's voice coming from it, making me jump.

'Drink up your Ovaltine, Carol Anne, and then get off to bed or you'll be tired in the morning.'

'Oh, not yet, Mum,' came Carol Anne's usual whingey tones. 'I'm not a bit tired.'

'Do as your mother tells you,' ordered Mr Perkins' disembodied voice, followed by a rebellious muttering from Carol Anne.

Polly switched off the radio and looked at me triumphantly.

'Well?'

'Well what?' I said blankly. 'How d'you do that? Can they hear us too?'

Polly shook his head.

'No. It gave me ever such a shock tonight when I first picked them up on the radio like that. But I've worked it out now. It's that pen.'

'Pen?' I repeated.

'Yeah. The one Sam found. I'd left it on the table in the lounge. It must be a bug.'

'Don't be daft,' I said. 'It's just a pen.'

'It is. But it's also a bug. It must be. They're getting quite popular. Look here.'

He thrust a magazine under my nose, pointing eagerly to the open page, at the top of which was a picture of a hand holding a pen exactly like the one we'd found. Over the top was a headline:

DO YOU WANT TO KNOW A SECRET?

'These pens are being used by top businessmen,' said Polly importantly. 'Industrial espionage it's called. They leave the pen lying on a desk in the boardroom, then they go into another room, tune in the radio and overhear all the secrets from the boardroom. The magazine says it's being done all the time.'

'Cor! And we've got it.' My agile mind began to dredge up all sorts of delightful possibilities. 'We could put it in the staffroom at school and—'

'I'm not getting into anything like that.' Polly had paled visibly. 'We'd get ourselves sacked if they caught us. No. I just thought it might come in useful for a case.'

I came reluctantly back to earth.

'Suppose you're right. Tell you what – let's take it to the zoo in Camcaster on Saturday. I bet there's all sorts of crooks hanging about there.'

'Yeah. OK.' Polly's face cleared. 'Is Sam coming with us? I bet she'd be interested. And she was the one who found the pen.'

'We'll brief her tomorrow,' I decided. 'I'd better get off now. It's nearly curfew time. Just switch the thing on again for a sec and see what we get.'

Polly obeyed. Almost immediately his mother's voice came through.

'I'd better go up and give those two a knock. It's nearly nine.'

'See what I mean?' I said, hastily grabbing my anorak. 'See you tomorrow, mate.'

Mrs Perkins and I met on the stairs.

123

'Must be going,' I said cheerily. 'Don't want to be late.'

'That's a good boy.' Mrs Perkins sounded astonished that this should be the case. 'Good night, James.'

''Night, Mrs Perkins,' I smarmed greasily and oiled my way out.

We explained the affair to Sam on the way to school next morning. It's not easy to convey complicated information when you're cycling along in heavy traffic. But we managed. Just. Sam was all agog.

'Lordy! It's just the sort of thing vigilantes like us should have. Yeah, I'll tag along to the zoo with you on Saturday. We'll have a great time. I bet there's dozens of crooks planning bank raids and things in a place like the zoo.'

'And spies,' broke in Polly. 'They often meet in zoos, you know, to give away secrets and sell info to the enemy. There was that film on telly only last week —'

He broke off as a loud hooting from a car behind us forced us back into single file. Its driver shook his fist and mouthed abuse as he passed us. I gave him a cheerful wave. It was not returned.

My dad seemed quite to approve of the idea of the zoo visit. He said he was glad I was taking an intelligent interest in things at last. Sam, of course, can usually terrorize her oldies into submission, while even Polly's pair raised no objections to a nice educational afternoon observing the world's wildlife and Polly's dad bought him a new film for his camera. Moreover he coerced them into agreeing that he might come home to tea with me after the zoo visit. Polly always welcomes this as a real perk. It gives him a much-appreciated break from the vegetarian, high fibre diet his mum inflicts on him at home.

It was just before two thirty that the three of us tumbled eagerly off the bus in the zoo car park, paid our entrance fee and wandered in.

Camcaster Zoo is terrific. It's really more like a sort of wildlife park. The animals are in enclosures, but they've all got oodles of space and appear pretty well-fed and contented. Even without any crooks around it looked like being a sponditious afternoon.

We ambled around for a bit, dividing our attention between the animals and possible suspicious characters, but most of the visitors seemed to be law-abiding families with hordes of kids in tow. We did see a likely couple of men sitting on a bench, who, we all thought, could be plotting villainy. So we drew lots as to who should plant the pen on the seat by them. I drew the short straw as it were. Polly handed me the pen. I took a deep breath then began to creep silently (and nervously) across the grass. The two men, I thought bitterly, could probably hear my heart thumping as I approached. I reached the bench and cautiously slid the pen onto the end of it. As I straightened, one of the men turned round.

'What're you up to, lad?'

It never ceases to amaze me the way grown-ups always seem to think you're 'up to something'. I gave him my honest, open, Boys' Own Paper type smile.

'Dropped my hanky. It blew under the seat.'

The guy grunted and turned back to his companion. I returned to Sam and Polly, who were busy holding their breath behind the nearest bush.

'Device in position and activated,' I reported.

'Gosh!' said Polly. 'You did that jolly well, JB. Really cool. I thought they'd rumbled you.'

'Piece of cake,' I assured him. 'Well, get on with it. We may be missing vital info here.'

'Right.' Polly switched on the radio and fiddled about with the tuner. Suddenly a man's voice came through.

'They can't hold a candle to Liverpool I tell you. No way.'

'Dunno,' said a lighter voice. 'Got some good goal scorers, United have. Reckon they've a chance of the cup next season. They're on the way up. You see if I'm not right.'

'Nah.' The other man was dismissive. 'If you ask me—'

Polly switched off. We looked at each other.

'Football!' said Sam disgustedly. 'We might have known. *They're* a dead loss, anyway.'

Polly said, 'We gotta get my pen back off that seat.'

He looked at me. Sam looked at me. It was obvious who was going to have to get the pen. I sighed.

'OK. If they start anything, ring the cops.'

I made my way across to the seat, edged up and reached out a tentative hand for the pen. The nearest man turned round, saw who it was and glared at me as if he were considering phoning Rentokil.

'You again! What is it this time?'

I gaped at him for a second, then my brain went into overdrive. I picked up the pen.

'Must have dropped this when I bent down to pick up my hanky. Lucky I spotted it was gone. It was a present.'

'Careless little brute,' snapped the man and turned away showing no further interest. I made my escape.

'I'm sick of this,' said Polly, shoving the pen back into his top pocket. 'Let's go and talk to the chimps.'

'Let's get ice creams first,' suggested Sam.

This met with unanimous approval, so we bought three ice cream cornets and, sucking loudly and appreciatively, followed the signs leading to the chimps' enclosure.

'Charley's here, you know,' said Sam. 'He's on loan temporarily.'

I looked at her blankly.

'Charley?'

'Yeah. You know. Does that advert on telly. The "Anyone for coffee?" one.'

'Oh him,' I said. 'He's great. Outacts all the humans. Wonder if we'll recognize him.'

We found the chimps without difficulty and stood eyeing them with interest. The interest appeared to be mutual. Several chimps swung across and hung on the bars, chattering to us excitedly. Sam pointed.

'That's Charley.'

'How d'you know?' I said.

'He's got a scar on his hand. See – there. I've noticed it on telly.'

Charley gave an amiable squawk and stretched out a hand through the bars.

'He wants some ice cream,' said Polly. 'Look – he's reaching out for it. I'll see if he'll take it off me. I can easily get another.'

He moved as close as he could get to the bars. Charley shot out a hand towards him and grabbed.

'Ow!' said Polly. 'No, you fool. You can't have that. That's mine.'

Too late. It wasn't the ice cream cornet which had taken Charley's fancy. It was the pen. And what was more, he'd got it, having snatched it with all the skill of a professional pickpocket. Polly held out a hand to retrieve it. Chattering excitedly, Charley retreated to the back of the enclosure and examined his prize with interest. Polly, as usual, looked at me for guidance.

'What shall I do now, JB? I must get it back.'

'We'd best find a keeper,' said Sam. 'Come on.'

'It was your own fault,' a woman holding a baby told Polly triumphantly. 'No sense, some kids.'

I gave her a glare which could have corroded copper and we hastily moved away before other members of the great British public joined in on the act.

You'd think there'd be keepers around all over the place in a zoo, wouldn't you? There aren't. At least, not this particular afternoon there weren't. We eventually found a depressed looking girl, who listened sympathetically, but then told us she couldn't do anything because she was reptiles. She did, however, direct us to the zoo office, where, she assured us, they would be able to help.

128

'Don't tell them it's a bug,' I instructed Polly as we set off. 'You know how funny grown-ups can be. Just say it's an ordinary pen.'

'But expensive,' added Sam. 'And say it was a prezzie from your dad, so you gotta get it back or he'll kill you.'

Polly nodded earnestly.

At the office, we repeated our tale of woe to a small man with the face of a worried weasel. His expression became even more lugubrious as he listened.

'You won't get it back easy,' he assured us. 'Not off Charley, you won't. Little devil he is. Best wait till he loses interest in it.'

'And how long,' I said coldly, 'is that likely to be? We gotta catch the five o'clock bus.'

The man shrugged.

'Difficult to say. Tell you what, leave your name and address. I'll ask Charley's keeper to get the thing while Charley's having his supper tonight. Then we'll post it to you.'

So Polly wrote down his name and address and we thanked the weasel for his help and wandered off. Polly said, 'Let's just go back and see if Charley's still mucking about with my pen. Or if he's eaten it or something.'

There was, however, no sign of Charley in the chimps' enclosure, though the rest of the chimps seemed to be unusually restive and unsettled.

'He must have gone into that house thing they've got at the back,' said Sam. 'Let's go round behind it and see if you can pick up any sounds on the radio.'

'Good idea.' Polly brightened. 'We ought to hear something. Even if he's only rustling about in the straw.'

But the radio, though obligingly giving us all the stations one after the other, refused to pick up any sound from Charley. I frowned at Polly.

'Sure you're doing it right?'

''Course I am,' said Polly indignantly. 'I bet he's eaten the thing.'

'Wouldn't it register noises inside him as it sort of went down?' I said.

Polly eyed me coldly.

'Not if he's chewed it up it wouldn't. I hope he's OK.'

'Well,' said Sam practically, 'we can't do any more here. Let's go and get the bus home. It's getting on for five.'

The zoo bus stand is at one end of the car park and the bus then travels to the bus station in Camcaster, from where we could get another one home. We ambled across the car park, with Polly still messing about with his radio and producing occasional blaring music, intermingled with what appeared to be a commentary on a horse race. Suddenly there was another sound on the radio, quite different from anything we'd heard previously. It sounded exactly like someone snoring. Polly came to a halt.

'That's funny!' he said.

'Atmospherics, I expect,' I said knowledgeably.

Polly shook his head.

'Not atmospherics. And I'm getting it on the same wavelength as I had the pen. Funny. We're a long way from the chimps here. I shouldn't think the bug'd pick up anything at this distance.'

'Let's walk around a bit and see if it gets louder or anything,' Sam suggested.

We wandered over to our left. The snoring promptly became so faint we could hardly hear it. We turned right. The snoring got louder.

'It's this way all right,' said Sam. 'Keep going.'

We kept going. So did the snores. They led us to the far end of the car park, a secluded area where a board announced in large letters: PARKING FOR ZOO STAFF ONLY. We finished up beside a small blue van. There was no doubt that the snores were coming from inside the back of it.

'Funny!' said Polly again. 'D'you suppose Charley's asleep in there?'

'How could he be?' I said scornfully.

'Well, if he isn't there, my pen is.' Polly sounded stubborn. 'And it isn't the pen snoring.'

'Perhaps they're taking Charley to the vet,' suggested Sam.

'With zoos, the vet visits *them*,' I told her knowledgeably. 'Don't you remember that series on telly?'

'What are you kids up to?' snapped a man's voice. 'If you're vandalizing my van, there'll be trouble.'

We spun round like three puppets controlled by a singularly jumpy puppeteer. Behind us stood a man. At first sight he didn't look a particularly terrifying figure. He was medium height and bespectacled and obviously one of these office bods because he carried a small briefcase. He reminded me of one of our more inoffensive teachers. That is, he did until I took a closer look and saw the eyes

131

behind the spectacles. If you can imagine a teddy bear with the eyes of a killer shark, you've got the picture. The crocs in the reptile house had looked more friendly. I gave him the sort of placating little smile I usually reserve for boy-eating teachers.

'We weren't touching your van, sir,' I grovelled. 'Just going for the bus.'

'The bus,' said the guy coldly, 'stops right over on the other side of the car park.'

Polly decided, unwisely, to enter the conversation.

'You see we thought we heard – OW!'

The 'OW' was because I'd stamped on his foot.

'Thought you heard – what?' The Killer Shark was beginning to gaze at us like Dracula looking for a throat. I said hastily, 'A kitten. We thought we heard a kitten. Over here. Mewing. So we came. But it – er – ran off.'

'Mmm!' The man eyed us thoughtfully. We stared back with innocent, expressionless stares. He gave up.

'Well – get off for your bus then. Go on. Scarper.'

We scarpered obediently and with such enthusiasm that lemmings would have been trampled in the rush. Behind us we heard the van start up. I risked a quick glance over my shoulder. To my relief, the van was not following us with murderous intent, but was moving in the opposite direction. Nevertheless, we didn't stop running until we reached the bus stop, where a queue of people were already shuffling slowly on to the bus.

Once safely seated on the nice long seat at the

back, Sam produced her diary and scribbled something in it. I looked at her curiously.

'What're you doing?'

'Noting the number of that van,' said Sam promptly. 'You never know.'

Polly said, 'I know my pen was inside it anyway.'

'And that guy was a villain if ever I saw one,' I said. 'Did you see the way he looked at us?'

'Scary,' agreed Sam.

We discussed the matter all the way home and were still chewing it over when we got off the bus in Elwich town centre and began to walk slowly along the street. Suddenly Polly said, 'Hey! Isn't that the van?'

We came to a halt. I looked at him.

'Which van?'

'The one at the z-zoo. The b-blue one. Look!'

He was pointing down a narrow side street on our right. It was a quiet cul-de-sac, with lock-up garages down one side and a disused warehouse at the other. At the far end large double gates opened on to a cobbled yard. The gates were wide open and in the yard stood a blue van. I eyed it uncertainly.

'Is it the same one?'

'Sure is.' Sam was consulting her diary. 'Same number. Come on.'

She set off determinedly in the direction of the van. With vivid memories of Killer Shark, I hesitated. Sam turned round.

'Scared?'

'Of course not,' I said coldly. 'Just thinking of the best way to—'

Sam snorted derisively. Polly was holding his

radio to his ear. He said, 'I've p-picked up the snoring on the radio again. It's f-faint but it's there.'

That settles it, I thought gloomily. Now we'll have to investigate.

'OK,' I said. 'But go canny. Don't just charge in.'

We crept cautiously down the street and peered round the side of the gates into the yard.

Except for the van the yard was empty. But the snoring was definitely louder.

'It's not c-coming from the v-van.' Polly sounded puzzled. 'It's over on the left. Listen!'

We listened.

'Polly's right.' Sam sounded excited. 'It's coming from those outbuildings.'

A dilapidated low building bordered the left side of the yard. It looked as if it could once have been stables, but had now fallen into disuse. I gave a quick glance round. Everywhere was deserted. From the main road could be heard the muted but reassuring sound of traffic. I took a deep breath.

'OK. Let's have a dekko.'

We crossed to the building at a crouching nervous run. The snoring grew clearer by the minute.

'My p-pen's in there all right,' said Polly with certainty.

Sam was examining the door.

'I don't reckon it's locked,' she said triumphantly. 'Just bolted top and bottom. Make a back, Polly. I can't reach the top bolt.'

Polly bent down obediently. Sam scrambled up and slid back the top bolt while I did the same for the lower one. Cautiously we eased the door open and edged inside.

On some straw in one of the stalls lay a chimpanzee, fast asleep and snoring gently. By his side was a bowl of water. His right hand lay on his chest. And beneath his fingers I could see the pen. I retrieved it gently and handed it to Polly.

'That's Charley,' Sam said. 'Look. You can see the scar on his hand.'

Polly, storing the pen carefully in his pocket, said, 'What shall we d-do now?'

The answer to that was I didn't know. Sam said, 'We gotta get him away. Can we wake him, d'you think? He's too big and heavy to carry.'

I was looking round the stable hoping for inspiration. My eye fell on something in the far corner.

'Hang on,' I said. 'Isn't that a wheelbarrow?'

I scurried across to it. It was indeed a wheelbarrow. One long past its sell-by date but still apparently in working order. Just. I seized the handles and trundled it, creaking and groaning protestingly, back to the snoring Charley.

'Let's lift him into this,' I said.

'And then what?' Polly sounded mutinous.

'Straight to the nick,' I said. 'It's not far.'

It might not have been far but, by the time we'd manhandled the still placidly snoring Charley into the barrow and trundled the barrow from the yard to the cul-de-sac and from the cul-de-sac to the High Street, it began to seem a very long way indeed.

For one thing Charley was no lightweight. For another, the barrow appeared to be drunk and kept staggering from side to side, taking with it whoever was pushing it at the time. And thirdly we were plagued by the obvious interest of passing pedestrians, who seemed to think the whole thing a bit odd.

'It'll be Jeremy Beadle and that lot,' I heard one old man say authoritatively.

'Either that or Esther Rantzen,' agreed another guy.

'Isn't that the chimp who's in the advert?' A woman with a yelling baby in a pram had decided to add her quota. 'Perhaps they're doing a new one.'

'Can you see the TV cameras?' another voice queried.

Red-faced and embarrassed, we ploughed on.

Suddenly Polly said anxiously, 'I think we're being f-followed.'

'Yeah,' I said bitterly. 'By half of Elwich.'

'N-no.' Polly's voice emerged as a squeak that a terrified hamster might have envied. 'By HIM.'

Sam darted a hasty glance over her shoulder.

'Yikes! The guy from the zoo. He's seen us.'

I looked back. The Killer Shark was there all right – some way behind us but overtaking fast.

'Run!' I said urgently.

Easier said than done. We tried of course. But it was hopeless. Killer Shark was unencumbered. We had a large, doped chimp in a drunken wheelbarrow. No contest. Next second I felt a hand on my shoulder.

'Just a minute, lad,' a voice grated.

Still clutching the handles of the barrow, I cast

a terrified glance upwards. Killer Shark, with the expression of a lion working up an appetite for his next Christian, eyed me malevolently.

'Where are you taking that chimp?' he demanded.

'The nick,' I said bravely. 'You stole him.'

A crowd was beginning to gather. Sam appealed to them.

'That man,' she said, pointing dramatically to Killer Shark, 'kidnapped Charley from the zoo this afternoon.'

A low, threatening rumble came from the crowd. They all knew and loved Charley. The man glared round.

'It's a lie,' he yelled. 'These kids took him. I'm taking him back. Hand him over.'

He tried to wrest the barrow from my grasp. I hung on. Sam seized his wrists in a judo grip. Polly, dancing about on the sidelines, attempted to hack the guy's shins. The crowd howled encouragement but offered no help. Typical, I thought.

Things suddenly began to happen rather quickly. There was a screech of brakes as a passing police patrol car drew up and two cops leapt out to investigate the disturbance.

'What's all this then?' said one, shouldering his way through the crowd.

His sidekick said excitedly, 'Hey Sarge, that's Charley. You know, we just got the call on the radio saying he'd been snatched. That's him!'

'Well, well, well!' The sergeant, obviously scenting promotion, proceeded to take charge. In no time at all, the crowd had been dispersed, police

reinforcements called up and we, together with
Charley, were on our way to the nick in one police
car, while Killer Shark, under guard, travelled in
another.

They were expecting us at the nick. A cop carried
off the still snoring Charley to await the arrival of
the zoo vet with transport. Killer Shark was
escorted off to be questioned – with, I hoped, a
judicious use of thumbscrews. And Sam, Polly and
I told the whole story to a group of admiring cops.
The entire thing was fab! Then Sam's dad arrived,
having been contacted by one of his mob and, after
lashings more praise from the fuzz and the hint that
we might even get a reward from the zoo, he loaded
us all into his car to take us home.

There was just one snag. When we proudly and
unwarily showed him the bug/pen, Sam's dad said
sharply, 'Where did you get that?'

'I found it,' said Sam. 'Then I swapped it with
Polly for a Jason Donovan single. I thought it was
just a pen.'

'And Polly found it was a bug,' I said. 'He's a
real whizz like that.'

'And I'm going to confiscate it,' said Sam's dad.
'It's not a toy and it doesn't really belong to you.
It could also lead to trouble. Hand it over.'

Polly reluctantly obeyed. I mean, you can't argue
with a top cop, can you? Sam tried to protest, but
was swiftly quelled.

Mr Spencer dropped us all off at my gate before
driving back to the nick. We stood there despon-
dently.

'Honestly!' I said. 'Grown-ups! That pen was just

138

what we needed to suss out crooks. Think he'll change his mind?'

'Dad never changes his mind.' Sam sounded gloomy.

'Oh well,' said Polly, 'we've done OK up to now without the thing. You're better at sussing out crooks than any old pen, JB.'

I smiled smugly.

'You're not so bad yourself. Either of you,' I added hastily, as I caught Sam's eye.

Sam gave that Mona Lisa type smile of hers that she knows never fails to irritate me.

'Thanks a bundle, she said sarcastically.

8
The Single Shoe Mystery

Just as the snoring chimp affair stemmed from Sam finding the pen/bug, so a month later our next case began when Polly's dog, Whisky, found a shoe.

Now Whisky, although part golden retriever, has rarely been known to retrieve anything. Throw a ball for him and he comes back without it, and more or less accuses you of only pretending to throw. So the fact that he did retrieve the shoe made us take the thing seriously from the start.

Polly and Sam and I had been spending Saturday afternoon taking Whisky for a long walk over Farrington's fields. Actually I was pretty glad of the excuse to escape from the house for the afternoon. This was because Susan, my drippy older sister, had decided to honour us with one of her rare weekend visits. Thankfully, we don't very often see her, or her endless succession of boyfriends, as she's away at university most of the time. But when she does come home she tends to disrupt the entire household and, as I never seem to be able to do anything right as far as she's concerned, I find it better to keep out of her way as much as possible.

Anyway, to get back to Whisky and the shoe.

Once on Farrington's fields – which is a stretch of common land outside town bordering the local golf course – we let Whisky off his lead and he pranced off on one of his usual rabbit hunts. He's never caught a rabbit, mind you, but I'll say one thing for him, he keeps on trying with a dogged persistence worthy of better things.

After he'd disappeared into the middle distance we played around for a bit with an enormous new kite which Polly's doting oldies had bought him. It was a pretty super kite, but there wasn't really enough wind to do it justice and it had just sunk dispiritedly to the ground for the third time when Polly said, 'Gosh! Looks like Whisky's caught something at last.'

Whisky was hurtling towards us like a demented flying saucer, gripping something in his jaws. The something stuck out blackly at each side of his jowls like a Mexican type moustache. And his face wore a look of smug satisfaction.

He slid to a halt in front of us and laid his offering proudly at Polly's feet, then stood back wagging his tail frantically and waiting for the round of applause.

'It's a shoe,' said Polly blankly.

'I can see that,' I agreed. 'Question is, where'd he get it?'

'It's not,' said Sam thoughtfully, 'the sort of shoe you'd wear for tramping over the fields.'

It wasn't. It was a woman's shoe, a black, strappy sandal with a very high thin heel which would have snapped off after five minutes on the rough ground. I bent and picked it up.

'More a party type of thing,' I said judicially. 'Our Sue's got a pair like this. She wears them to go nightclubbing.'

'So where'd Whisky pick it up?' said Polly.

Sam said, 'Lordy! D'you suppose he's found a dead body? It was on the news only the other night where a girl was murdered and a man walking his dog found her. D'you think—'

I looked at her in sudden realization.

'I bet you're right. I mean, that sort of thing's happening all the time these days, isn't it?'

'So what are we going to d-do?' Polly was beginning to stammer so I knew he was getting het up. I was about to answer when Sam, as usual, beat me to it. She said, 'Get Whisky to lead us to the body, of course. Then we can pinpoint the place for the cops.'

'M-must we?' said Polly plaintively. 'I mean, the body could be AWFUL. D-dismembered or something. I d-don't want—'

'Don't be such a wimp,' I said severely. 'We're supposed to be vigilantes, aren't we? Got to get used to horrors. Give Whisky the shoe and tell him to lead us to the owner. Go on.'

To be honest, I wasn't too keen myself on viewing mutilated corpses, but I had no intention of saying so. Not with Sam standing there waiting for any sign of weakness, I wasn't. I waggled the shoe I was holding under Whisky's nose.

'Find!' I said encouragingly. 'Good boy. Find.'

Whisky seized the shoe and began to worry it, growling playfully. I looked at Polly.

'Can't you make the thicko understand?'

'He's not thick,' said Polly indignantly. 'He's a very intelligent dog. He—'

'Then get on with it, the pair of you,' said Sam impatiently.

Polly gave her a look which could have shattered bulletproof glass, then turned to Whisky.

'Good dog!' he crooned. 'Clever boy. Find. Come on. Find.'

I've noticed before that Polly and his dog seem to be on the same wavelength, as it were. Whisky, after eyeing his master thoughtfully for a second, picked up the shoe and trotted off with it.

'Tally-ho!' said Sam triumphantly. 'Follow him.'

Polly picked up his kite and we pelted in pursuit.

Whisky, now moving like a heat seeking missile, headed straight across the common towards the far end, where a dense patch of bushes and trees marked its boundary with the golf course. At the edge of the shrubbery he paused to give us an encouraging glance, then plunged into the bushes. I halted.

'D'you suppose he's having us on?'

''Course not,' Polly said vehemently. 'He understands every word I say to him. But d'you think there is a b-body in there?'

'Only one way to find out,' said Sam and edged cautiously into the undergrowth. I followed, with Polly a reluctant third.

Whisky was waiting for us in a small clearing. He sat there, the shoe still in his mouth and a sort of pleased grin on his face. A quick glance round reassured me that there was, at least, no battered body in sight. There was, however, another shoe. It appeared to be the partner of the one Whisky still held. As we came to a halt, Whisky dropped

143

his shoe by its fellow and uttered a triumphant bark.

'Good boy!' said Polly. 'See, you pair, I told you. He led us straight to the other shoe.'

'Yeah,' I said. 'But what are the shoes doing here anyway?'

'Perhaps someone's chucked 'em out,' said Polly.

'No, they've not.' Sam had picked up the shoes to examine them. 'See. They've just been mended – you don't have shoes mended and then chuck them out. I bet there's a woman's body somewhere, shoved in the bushes maybe. And her shoes fell off as she was dragged in.'

'Or as she tried to escape,' I said.

'Perhaps she *did* escape,' said Polly hopefully.

'We gotta make sure,' I said. 'Search the bushes. You go that way and—'

Polly looked at me in horror.

'On my *own*? Suppose there is a body and the k-killer's still there? *LURKING*!'

I hesitated. I hadn't thought of that possibility. And I didn't much like it now it had been brought to my attention.

'Perhaps we'd better keep together,' I said uncertainly.

'Yeah,' agreed Sam. 'And go carefully. Just in case.'

'Good thinking,' I said. 'Come on, then.'

For the next few minutes, growing ever more jumpy and scared, we scoured those rotten bushes for mutilated corpses, while Whisky padded about getting in our way, terrifying us by rustling about

144

in the undergrowth and convincing himself he was helping.

We found nothing. Apart, that is, from a brown paper bag, which Polly unearthed from some brambles. He eyed it cautiously.

'D'you suppose it's a clue?'

'More likely had someone's lunch in it,' I said.

Polly shook his head.

'Too clean. I'll hang on to it in case.'

'The Body in the Bunker,' said Sam suddenly.

I gazed at her in irritation.

'What you on about?'

'That Agatha Christie thing. On telly. Last week. Remember? They found a body on the golf course. In a bunker.'

'Yeah,' I said. 'I remember now. D'you suppose—'

'I'm not,' said Polly with determination, 'walking all over the golf course lugging this kite. Besides, people'll be playing. They'll bawl us out. And anyway, they'd have found any dead body already. Bound to notice a thing like a dead body. Even when they're playing golf. I'm not going.'

We looked at him. His face was set and about as cheerful as a Roman coin. I capitulated.

'OK. But just let's have a dekko at the nearest bunker. See – through those trees.'

'I bet that's the one,' said Sam with enthusiasm. 'I mean, the killer wouldn't want to drag his victim right across into the open. She's probably lying there with her throat cut and—'

'I think I'm g-going to be sick.' Polly had paled visibly.

'Don't be so wet,' I said impatiently. 'Put Whisky on his lead. They don't like dogs loose on the golf course. And come on.'

Polly scowled at me.

'How many hands d'you think I've got? Put Whisky on his lead, carry the kite—'

'I'll take the kite,' I said, snatching it impatiently. 'Now, come on.'

Sam, obviously eager to see her first dismembered corpse, was already halfway to the bunker. Burdened by the kite, which was fast becoming a liability, I scurried after her, scared, but determined to rebut any accusation of being chicken. Polly brought up the rear, with Whisky tugging him eagerly forward.

The bunker was empty. Only Sam appeared disappointed.

'That's it then,' I said in relief. 'Satisfied?'

Sam eyed me in disgust.

'Call yourself a detective? Sherlock Holmes'd never leave a case half-finished like this. Those shoes must be a clue. And there must be a body. Somewhere.'

'Then l-let someone else find it,' said Polly sulkily.

'Tell you what,' I said, 'we'll take the shoes home with us. Then, if there's a report of a woman's body being found—'

'Or a girl gone missing,' interrupted Sam.

'Yeah. That too. Watch the news on telly. Then, if there's anything, we take the shoes to the cops. That way we won't look silly. And they won't just sneer.'

'Good idea,' said Sam. 'Got a hanky?'

I stared at her.

'A hanky? What for?'

'To pick up the shoes. There may be the murderer's fingerprints on them.'

How she thought any prints would have survived Whisky carrying the shoes around in his mouth I couldn't think. I told her so.

'You never know,' said Sam mysteriously. 'Forensic's wonderful. Dad says so.'

You can't argue with someone whose father's a top cop, can you? I gave in.

'OK. Where are the shoes anyway?'

'You left them in the bushes,' said Polly. 'I thought it was silly at the time,' he added self-righteously.

We charged back into the bushes.

The shoes were still there, waiting for us. Whisky promptly went into his On Guard position beside them. I looked at Polly.

'Give us your hanky, mate.'

'Why me?' Polly was showing signs of rebellion.

'Because you're the only one of us who ever has one. Hand it over.'

Polly reluctantly obeyed. I put the kite on the ground and carefully picked up the shoes, holding them in the hanky as I'd seen cops do so often on telly. Then I looked at the others.

'I'm going to look a right Charlie carrying them home like this.'

'You could, of course,' said Polly distantly, 'put them in this paper bag I found.'

'Brill!' I said. 'Give it here.'

With Polly and Sam holding the bag open, I inserted the shoes.

'Right,' I said. 'Polly, here's your hanky. Sam—'

'Shut up!' Sam's voice was urgent. 'Listen. There's someone coming.'

We listened.

The sound of feet trampling and crackling through the undergrowth came quite clearly to our ears. And it was getting nearer.

'The m-murderer!' Polly, ever one to look on the black side, was heading for panic stations. 'He's coming b-back.'

'Hide!' I gasped. 'Quick.'

After a second's thought I shook the shoes from the bag and dropped them on the ground in case the murderer was returning to look for them. Then, quickly stuffing the empty bag into my pocket, I dived into the undergrowth after the others. There we crouched, hardly daring to breathe and with our eyes fixed on the clearing.

Unfortunately Whisky had other ideas. For some reason best known to himself, Whisky appeared to think we had forgotten the shoes (which I hadn't) and the kite (which I had). Jerking his lead from Polly's grasp he plunged back into the clearing and picked up the kite in his mouth. He was just about to bring it back to us when a man emerged cautiously from the bushes at the other side of the clearing. Whisky, startled, sprang round to face him.

The newcomer was a young man, casually dressed in jeans and trainers and a white shirt, open at the neck. He didn't look like a villainous murderer, but then the murderer's always the most unlikely person, isn't it? All the telly serials insist on this. He slid to a halt as his eye fell on Whisky, who stood clutching his kite in a determined sort of way. Then his glance moved to take in the shoes. He made a satisfied sort of noise and darted across to pick them up.

Whisky gave a warning growl.

The man did an emergency stop with his hand on the shoes and looked at Whisky.

'Good doggie,' he said placatingly. Then, never taking his eyes off Whisky, he picked up the shoes with the same sort of movement a Roman emperor might have used when handing a tasty Christian to a rather tetchy lion.

'Good doggie,' he said again. 'See. I don't want your kite. I only want these. Good doggie.'

Whisky hesitated. Then he obviously decided to give the guy the benefit of the doubt. He stopped growling and wagged his tail.

'Good doggie,' the bloke repeated in relief.

Holding the shoes he backed away, then turned to hurry back the way he'd come.

'Gosh!' whispered Polly. 'He's disposing of the evidence.'

'Going to bury the shoes with the body,' agreed Sam. 'Come on. We gotta follow him.'

'Carefully,' I warned. 'Don't let him see us.'

Moving in single file we crept through the bushes in pursuit. It wasn't difficult. The guy obviously wasn't as used to playing Red Indians as we were. You could hear him a mile off. To my relief, even Whisky seemed to have understood the need for

149

silence. Still dragging the kite, he padded after Polly, with his tail wagging in obvious enjoyment of the chase.

Suddenly, ahead of us, we heard the man's voice.

'I've found them, darling,' he said. 'Bag must have blown away though.'

We paused, gazing at each other in bewilderment.

'Dominic! You angel!' It was a girl's voice and it sounded vaguely familiar. 'I'd only just collected them from the menders when I met you. And I need them to go clubbing tonight.'

I crept forward, moving in tracker fashion from tree to tree. We were, I noticed, approaching the end of the shrubbery where it bordered the golf course. Concealment would soon be impossible. Then the man's voice came again.

'There was a dog there. I thought he wasn't going to let me take them, but—'

'A dog?' said the girl's voice. 'What was a dog doing there?'

'Flying a kite, I think.' The man sounded uncertain.

The girl gave an affected little laugh.

'Dominic, darling, you are funny! I adore you.'

The voice was definitely familiar. I peered round my concealing tree.

Ahead of us lay the golf course. And at the edge of the course stood two figures clasped in each other's arms. No, that hardly does the scene justice. The pair were in a clinch so close it looked as though major surgery would be required to separate them. I recognized them both. One was the murderer we

150

had just seen collecting the shoes. The other was my sister, Susan.

Polly and Sam recognized her in the same moment. Polly gave a startled squeak. I clapped a hand over his mouth. Fortunately the couple were too occupied with each other to notice.

We remained frozen still, trying to come to terms with the changed scenario. Susan and the pseudo-murderer continued to embrace. She was looking at him, I observed, with the same expression Polly wears when he sights a fresh cream meringue. Sam nudged me.

'Best not let them see us. What d'you think?'

I nodded agreement and signalled 'Retreat' to Polly. Unfortunately, once again we had reckoned without Whisky.

Whisky likes our Susan. She feeds him with an endless succession of choccy bickies whenever she sees him and a choccy bicky was obviously something he really fancied at this moment. He dropped the kite and leapt forward with a joyous yelp, dragging Polly with him at the end of the lead and with the kite's string somehow entangled round his rear.

Susan gave a startled cry as Whisky leapt at her. She and Dominic sprang apart. Dominic's eyes fell on Whisky and he did a double take.

'Good Lord!' he exclaimed. 'It's the kite-flying pooch.'

My sister's gaze changed to an Arctic glare as she recognized Polly, who was standing clutching Whisky's lead and staring at the scene with the boiled codfish expression he habitually adopts at moments of stress.

151

'Paul Perkins,' she hissed accusingly, 'what are you doing here?'

'I – I – I—' Polly was obviously incapable of thinking what he might be doing.

'There's more kids in those bushes.' Dominic appeared to be staring straight at us. 'Come on out of it!'

He took a threatening step forward. Shame-facedly Sam and I emerged into the clearing. Susan took one look at me and let out a screech worthy of a banshee with toothache.

'James! Are you spying on me?'

'No. Honest,' I protested. 'I just—'

'You know this kid too?' asked Dominic disbelievingly.

'My beastly kid brother,' snapped Susan. 'And if you weren't spying, James, just what are you doing here?'

'It was the shoes,' I explained desperately. 'We found the shoes. At least Whisky did. They were lying around, see? And we thought p'raps the owner had been murdered and—'

Dominic began to laugh.

'And when you saw me come back for the shoes, you cast me in the role of first murderer, I suppose?'

'Something like that,' I muttered, furious that we'd been made to look such dumbos.

Dominic continued to chuckle.

'Sorry to disappoint you all. Anyway, no harm done and—'

'No harm done!' Susan's voice was still pitched several decibels higher than usual. 'Don't you realize that my young brother has all the tact normally associated with a cosh? I can imagine my parents' reaction when he tells the story over tea tonight. And he'll make the most of it. Then you'll walk in to take me clubbing and – well – it'll be so embarrassing.'

'Hmmm! I see the problem.' Dominic eyed me thoughtfully. 'Could you be persuaded to forget you saw your sister this afternoon, James?'

I had one of my sudden inspirations. Perhaps, after all, this disastrous situation could be turned to our advantage. I stared expressionlessly at Dominic.

'I might,' I said. 'If – er—' I paused meaningly.

'Blackmail, eh?' Dominic produced a pound coin from the pocket of his jeans and proffered it. I eyed it in silence. After a moment a second coin joined the first.

'There's three of us,' I said stonily.

Dominic silently added another coin to the two lying in his palm.

'How's that?'

The bargaining, I felt, was starting to resemble a street bazaar in Cairo. Any minute now he'd be throwing in a free holiday to Disneyland.

'Well . . . ' I said hesitantly.

'Three's my final offer.' Dominic was beginning to sound dangerous. I decided not to push my luck.

'OK. Done.' I said, stretching out my hand for the coins. 'And don't worry. My lips are sealed.'

'They'd better be,' said Dominic coldly. 'Now get the hell out of here and take that kite-flying mongrel with you.'

It seemed diplomatic to obey. Offering placating

153

little smiles all round, we scuttled off. Once back on the open common we came to a halt.

'Well,' said Polly disgustedly, 'that was a wash-out if ever I saw one. A murder, you two said. I thought at the time—'

'Oh, stop moaning,' I said. 'We got three quid out of it, didn't we? Equal shares, of course.'

'Of course,' said Sam. 'You know, I've been thinking. This vigilante lark pays pretty well, doesn't it? Five quid off Fatso for recovering his Walkman—'

'Five quid each for finding the film in the Heinz beans can,' I said. 'To say nothing of the reward from the zoo for getting Charley back.'

'Yeah,' said Sam. 'That was brill. And three today. Not bad going.'

'We made fools of ourselves.' Wet blanket Polly again.

'No one'll ever know,' I told him. 'Susan and her latest aren't going to split on us, are they? So cheer up. Let's buy some crisps and stuff with our winnings.'

Polly brightened.

'OK. You're on. And perhaps soon we'll have a proper case.'

'You betcha life we will,' I promised.

9

The Persecuted Prince
Problem

After the single shoe fiasco our lives proved completely uneventful for a couple of weeks until we did at last get the 'proper case' I'd forecast. In fact, we were plunged into a situation where our skill as vigilantes really proved its worth.

Mind you, if Bugs Bunny, our wet and woebegone history teacher, whom I mentioned earlier, hadn't been off sick that day the whole thing would never have got off the ground. But absent he was and we were just lolling round his classroom waiting for some stand in to arrive and behaving in a way that would have made the builders of the Tower of Babel look like reasonable people, when the door was flung violently open and Bonzo Barker, our headmaster, stalked in.

He must have heard the racket as he approached along the corridor, because he was giving his usual impersonation of a volcano about to erupt. As he strode across to the teacher's desk he eyed us coldly and a silence fell, so intense you could have cut it with a knife. We all sat up, trying to look alert and intelligent and all that jazz, as Bonzo informed us that he was about to take the lesson himself. One creep was even heard to murmur, 'Oh goody!'

There's one thing about Bonzo though. When he does actually teach he's dead interesting and he sure knows his stuff. And he'd chosen this lesson to talk about the Union Jack and how it came into being. Then he held up a small flag, having produced it apparently from his sleeve like a conjurer, and asked us what was wrong with it. No one knew. The thing looked perfectly OK to me. Our Susan's got a hideous T-shirt with the flag daubed all over the front and this looked exactly the same. We gazed at it in uneasy silence.

'Blind as bats, the lot of you.' Bonzo spoke in tones straight from the fast freeze shelf just as the continuing hush was becoming insupportable. 'Can you not see that I am holding your country's flag UPSIDE DOWN?'

I couldn't actually. Neither could anyone else apparently. However, Bonzo then explained how you could tell when it was the right way up, describing things so clearly that it made crystal seem opaque. As he finished the bell went and we all filed out in orderly fashion (very different from our usual exit) and went home. Apart from rejoicing that he hadn't set us any homework, we promptly forgot the whole thing. At least we thought we had. Only when you've heard something especially interesting bits tend to stick, don't they?

It was as we were on our way home from school the following Friday that Sam suggested we should all go into Camcaster the next day.

'Dad's got to go to a meeting at headquarters,' she said importantly, 'so he said he'd give us a lift in about nine thirty if we wanted to go. Only he doesn't know when he'll be through, so we'll have to get the bus back. You two keen?'

'Yeah,' I said. 'Sounds terrific. Maybe we'll get a chance at some vigilante stuff. Things have been a bit slow lately. Perhaps more doing in Camcaster.'

'Could be tomorrow,' said Polly unexpectedly. 'Hit men and hired killers and things.'

I looked at him.

'Why tomorrow especially? You got inside information or something?'

'I know what he's on about,' Sam broke in eagerly. 'It's that bloke's visit.'

'What bloke?' I asked blankly.

'The Thingummy of Whatsit.' Sam sounded unusually vague. 'You know, the crown prince of that African state. He's in Camcaster tomorrow. He's visiting the Tech 'cos some of his people are students there. And he's going to lunch and a meeting at the Town Hall. Then he's off to the Grosvenor factory in the afternoon. Dad says they're hoping to get a lot of orders from him. He likes England, see. He was at school here. It's been on telly on the news, JB. You must have seen it.'

'Oh – ah – yeah,' I said, with vague memories of a young, black, imposing looking guy being interviewed on his arrival in England. 'Touring all over the country looking at factories, isn't he? Wants to buy computers and machinery and stuff from us.'

'He'd do better buying guns,' Polly said solemnly. 'There's trouble in his country. A plot to overthrow him. It's led by his half-brother, Joachim.'

I looked at him irritably.

'Where d'you get all this gen?'

157

'I read the papers,' said Polly simply.

'Anyway,' said Sam, 'extra cops have been drafted in, Dad says, 'cos of the threats to his life. So Polly's right. There could be quite a bit of excitement around.'

'Great!' I said. 'OK. I'll be at your place by nine thirty. I'll brief the oldies tonight. How about you, Polly?'

'I *think* it'll be OK,' said Polly cautiously. 'If I tell them we're going with Mr Spencer and I don't mention about hit men. I'll sound Mum out over tea.'

'Ring me later then,' I said. 'And Sam, try to find what time this foreign guy's going to be at different places. Then we can be there too in case something exciting happens.'

Polly eyed me anxiously.

'Exciting like what?'

'Well – someone trying to shoot him or blow him up or–'

'I'm not going near any bombs.' Polly sounded quite definite on that point.

'We'll play it safe,' I assured him. 'Don't I always?'

Polly's expression became even more doubtful.

'It'll be quite safe,' said Sam. 'Dad'll be around anyway. But it'd be great if we could foil a rebel plot, wouldn't it? Wickedly megacool.'

I agreed, though privately I didn't really think anything exciting would happen. Not in sleepy old Camcaster, I didn't.

Polly rang me later to say he'd squared his oldies about the visit and the fact that they seemed quite happy about the whole thing reinforced my opinion that the day was likely to be completely uneventful. However, it was a day out, with a good, greasy nosh-up at McDonald's midday if we were lucky, so both Polly and I were waiting eagerly outside Sam's gate as she and her dad emerged next morning.

The drive to Camcaster wasn't particularly exciting. Mr Spencer's a good driver, but being a cop seems to limit him a bit and make him drive within speed limits and such. Still, he told us about some of his past cases and I suggested we might keep a lookout for this foreign VIP in case anything thrilling came up. Mr Spencer frowned.

'Not wise, James. There've been threats of trouble from a rebel faction in his own country. I'd prefer to think you three were out of it.'

I quickly pretended I'd lost interest and changed the subject before he started making us promise to keep away. I hate breaking promises and I fully intended that, if anything exciting were to happen, we would be there in the thick of it.

Inspector Spencer dropped us off outside cop headquarters, shouted, 'Have a good day,' and drove off. I turned to Sam.

'Right. Where's this Crown Prince Thingummy going to be first? Did you find out?'

'Yeah,' said Sam briefly. She glanced at her watch. 'He'll be at the Tech right now. I think our best bet is to be outside the Town Hall after lunch. He's due to leave there at two fifteen to drive to the Grosvenor works. We'd need a car to track him all round. At least the Town Hall's central.'

'S'pose you're right,' I said. 'OK. Let's go in the park for a bit, then have a snack at McDonald's and aim to get to the Town Hall steps just after two.'

'Brill!' said Polly. 'I've been looking forward to McDonald's ever since last night.'

As Polly's mum's still on her health food bonanza, a good nosh-up at McDonald's is the highlight of any day he spends in Camcaster. So we had our usual giant burgers and chips followed by apple pies followed by Cokes. Finally, stuffed to the brim, we waddled out and stood on the pavement outside. Sam looked at her watch.

'Getting on for two. Let's make for the Town Hall.'

'Don't expect me to run,' said Polly contentedly. 'Not after all that yummy-licious nosh.'

'Just walk quickly,' Sam encouraged. 'Do you good. Come on.'

We set off.

By ten past two we were in position at the foot of the short flight of steps leading to the imposing entrance to Camcaster Town Hall. I eyed the approach critically.

'Lots of chances for a sniper as that guy comes down the steps. Remember *The Day of the Jackal* on telly?'

'Yeah. So do the cops,' said Polly briefly. 'Look up there on the roof.'

Sam and I obeyed. Two cops armed with rifles were just visible above the parapet.

'Fab!' said Sam. 'Might be some action.'

'I hope they're good shots.' Polly sounded anxious. 'They might hit us by mistake if they're not c-careful.'

'Soon see,' I said callously. 'This looks like the guy's car arriving now.'

A large, highly polished, official looking vehicle, sporting a small Union Jack fluttering from the bonnet, was just drawing up at the foot of the steps. A liveried chauffeur leapt out smartly to hold open the rear door. At the same moment a small group of men emerged from the revolving doors of the Town Hall and came down the steps. I recognized the one in the middle from his picture on telly. The Crown Prince himself. I eyed him with interest. To my disappointment, he wasn't wearing royal robes. Just an ordinary lounge suit. In fact, he looked exactly like anyone else. Only as if he knew he wasn't, if you see what I mean.

But he did, I noticed, appear decidedly edgy. There seemed no doubt that he was taking the threats to his life seriously. He kept glancing round with a hunted sort of expression. His companions, whom I took to be bodyguards, were also on the alert. Two, in particular, kept their right hands in their pockets – probably grasping a revolver each, I reckoned – and eyed the street and surrounding buildings like hawks waiting to pounce. Nor was there any chatty leave-taking. The prince was hustled into the back of the car followed by his two armed guards, the chauffeur slammed the door behind them and moved swiftly back to the driver's seat. Slowly the car drew away from the kerb. The rest of the party, obviously realizing the show was over, relaxed visibly and moved back up the steps, chatting. They disappeared into the Town Hall.

'Well, that's it then,' I said disgustedly. 'About as exciting as playing Happy Families with the vicar at a church social.'

'Pity,' agreed Sam. 'I was hoping for a bit of action.'

'Yeah,' said Polly thoughtfully. 'Funny about the flag though.'

I frowned at him.

'What flag?'

'The one on the car. You'd think they'd be more careful.'

'Careful about what?' I said.

'The flag,' said Polly, as if that explained everything.

'What about it?' shrieked Sam and I in unison.

Polly gazed at us in surprise.

'Didn't you notice? They'd got it upside down.'

We came to a sudden halt and stared at him.

'It couldn't have been,' I said doubtfully.

'Are you sure?' said Sam at the same moment.

Polly nodded.

'Yeah. I'm sure. And it was. Remember, JB, Bonzo said—'

'I remember,' I said shortly. I cast my mind back. I recalled seeing the flag fluttering from the car bonnet, but apart from just registering that it was the Union Jack, I hadn't noticed it particularly. Of course, I hadn't Polly's advantages. As I've said before, he was a Cub Scout when he was a little kid and it still shows. I shrugged.

'Careless of them. Perhaps they thought foreigners wouldn't notice.'

Sam was looking quite excited.

'They wouldn't be that careless, JB. Dad says all our officials take the flag very seriously. I bet only a foreigner would ever make a mistake and put it upside down. I think there's something funny going on.'

'Like what?' I said blankly.

'Kidnap!' said Sam in sepulchral tones.

'The baddies have nobbled the prince,' amplified Polly. 'I told you there was an uprising against him. Probably they've taken him off somewhere quiet to kill him,' he added gloomily.

Sam spoke with determination. 'We'd better tell someone.'

She set off up the Town Hall steps. Reluctantly we followed. I, for one, was wondering if we weren't going to make utter fools of ourselves. But it's no good trying to stop Sam when she's got the bit between her teeth. You'd have as much luck as poor old Canute had when he started ordering the sea about.

At the top of the steps stood a man in a sort of commissionaire's uniform – bottle green with lashings of gold braid. He eyed us doubtfully. Sam ignored him and strode past to the revolving door. I followed, favouring him with my placating little smile. As Polly drew level with him, the guy weakly held out a hand to stop him.

'Where d'you three think you're going?'

'I'm with them,' said Polly hastily and barged

past. The poor wimp stared indecisively after us. Next second we were all through the door.

Just inside the doorway a group of men stood laughing and talking. I recognized most of them as the ones who'd just officiated at the prince's hurried departure. Sam stalked straight up to them.

'Excuse me,' she said in clear, carrying tones, 'but I think your Crown Prince has just been kidnapped.'

The men stopped talking. Their heads swung round towards Sam like the swivel mounts of guns on a tank turret. Undeterred as usual, Sam stared back. Eventually one of the group, a grey haired, civil servant type spoke.

'How did you get in here?'

Typical! I thought. Not a word of concern for the prince. Just the usual attitude of, it's kids so they must be up to something. I decided I'd better take over..

'You see,' I explained, 'it was the flag.'

'Upside down,' amplified Polly, nodding vigorously.

'So we knew they were fakes,' concluded Sam triumphantly.

One of the men in the group appeared to think this was a great joke. Civil Service type didn't. He had cold eyes, I noticed, and nothing much in the way of lips. He used the eyes now to give us the sort of look Medusa the Gorgon must have bestowed on her victims.

'Go away, you stupid children,' he said, 'or you'll be in serious trouble.'

164

'You don't understand,' I said desperately. 'We saw—'

There was an interruption. The wimpish commissionaire shot through the revolving doors as if jet propelled. Civil Service type transferred the Medusa glare to him.

'What is it, Blane?'

'The car,' babbled the commissionaire. 'The Crown Prince's car. It's just arrived. The chauffeur says he's sorry he's late. There was a traffic block.'

'Just *arrived*?' said Civil Service type blankly. 'But—'

'There you are,' said Sam, getting in the last word as usual. 'We told you. Your prince has been nobbled. '

'Impossible!' said Civil Service type.

'See for yourself.' Blane gestured sulkily towards the door. 'Car's standing there now.'

We all rushed outside to have a look. A car, the replica of the one which had borne away the Crown Prince a few minutes earlier, stood at the foot of the steps. Beside it, looking a bit bewildered, stood a man in chauffeur's uniform.

'Flag's the right way up this time,' said Polly's voice in my ear. 'This must be the proper car.'

I looked at the Union Jack fluttering proudly from the bonnet and used Bonzo's test on it. It was, indeed, right way up.

A bitter, three-sided argument appeared to be taking place between our group, led vociferously by Civil Service type, versus the chauffeur and the commissionaire. Everyone seemed to be blaming everyone else and looking for a scapegoat. Sam said loudly, 'The car was an H registration. It was exactly like this car. Don't you think you ought to get the cops on to it?'

A tall, slender man in the group swung round on her.

'Did you get the rest of the number?'

Sam shook her head.

'Not all of it. Five four something. I think.'

'The rest was muddied over,' Polly broke in. 'I thought that was funny too. Like the flag.'

'What's this about a flag?' The tall guy seemed genuinely interested.

'The one on the bonnet,' I explained. 'It was upside down.'

The tall guy nodded tersely, produced a mobile phone from his briefcase and began to call up reinforcements. That done, he started to cross-examine us to see if we'd noticed anything else. But, of course, we hadn't. So we found ourselves briefly thanked and then summarily dismissed.

We did hang around outside for a bit, but apart from a lot of coming and going and cops getting ever more thick on the ground, nothing very definite appeared to be happening. Moreover, it was beginning to rain. I looked at the others.

'Let's scarper, eh? Looks as if the baddies have got away with it.'

'I wonder if they'll kill him?' said Sam ghoulishly. 'The prince, I mean.'

'Probably hold him as a hostage,' I said knowledgeably.

'I wonder,' said Polly thoughtfully, 'how they did it?'

I looked at him irritably.

'We *saw* how they did it, moron. A fake car. That nobody spotted except us.'

'Except me,' said Polly. 'But I didn't mean that. I meant there were three of them. Even if the chauffeur was a phoney, the guy had his bodyguards with him and—'

I shrugged.

'I s'pose they were in the plot. Bribed probably. Anyway, there's nothing more to see here. Perhaps it'll be on the news tonight.'

'And Dad may have inside info,' said Sam hopefully. 'Come on. Race you to the bus station.'

We shot off. Sam won. As usual.

Over tea that evening I regaled my oldies with our adventures. They didn't seem too impressed. Dad just sniffed in disbelief and accused me of making it all up. I retaliated by challenging him to watch the news on telly and see if the kidnap were mentioned. He did and it was, though our part in the episode was ignored.

The fake car, the newsreader remarked chattily, had been found abandoned in a lonely country lane some miles outside Camcaster. In the back of the car traces of gas had been detected, together with a mechanism for feeding said gas through from the front of the car to the occupants of the rear seats. It seemed likely, therefore, concluded the newsreader triumphantly, that these occupants had been rendered unconscious.

'So that was how they did it,' I said aloud. 'We wondered.'

My father gave me a look about half a degree above freezing point.

'To hear you talk, James, we'll have MI5 hammering on the door any minute requesting your help.'

I put on my maltreated boy expression, but didn't attempt a reply.

Next morning I went round to the Spencers for my usual judo lesson from Sam's dad, but he wasn't there. All police leave had been stopped according to Sam.

'The cops are working full out on this Crown Prince lark,' she told me. 'They think he'll be smuggled out of the country. There's a watch on all ports and airports.'

'He could be dead and buried by now,' I protested.

Sam shook her head.

'Dad says not. The idea is to cart him back to his own country for a public trial and execution.'

'Charming!' I said. 'Oh well, nothing we can do. We tried. Look, Polly and I are taking Whisky walkies this afternoon. Wanna tag along?'

'OK,' said Sam agreeably.

'Pick you up at two then,' I said. 'Be ready.'

Prompt at two o'clock, therefore, the pair of us set off to Polly's pad. For once he was early and we met him on his way down Laurel Grove to meet us, with a docile Whisky walking on his lead beside him.

'Where shall we go?' asked Sam as soon as Whisky had shaken hands all round and wolfed the choccy bicky she offered as a reward.

'Let's hike over to Friary Woods,' said Polly promptly. 'It's one of Whisky's fave places. Because of the rabbits, see.'

We set off.

Once in the woods, we let Whisky off the lead and played hide and seek with him for a bit, before he galloped off on his own, woofing madly as if to declare that he could smell rabbits all over.

After that we messed around aimlessly waiting for him to return. Then suddenly, in the distance, we heard an agitated barking.

'That's Whisky,' said Polly with certainty. 'He's in trouble.'

'Come on,' I said.

We pelted off in the direction of the barks.

Friary Woods are intersected by numerous tracks and bridle paths. We raced along one of these, a rather wider one than usual. The sound of barking grew louder. All at once we emerged into a clearing and came to an abrupt halt. Our gallant retriever had made another find. Bigger than a shoe this time.

In the centre of the clearing was a dark green car and by it stood Whisky on his hind legs, pawing at the boot of the vehicle and barking at intervals.

We slid to a halt.

'Whisky!' said Polly uncertainly. 'What's up, boy?'

Whisky darted him one swift, apologetic glance, then pawed at the boot again and whined anxiously.

'Bet he's found a dead body,' said Sam. I've mentioned before this tendency she has to see crime everywhere.

'You've got dead bodies on the brain,' I said. 'More likely a family of rabbits.'

Sam eyed me scornfully.

'Rabbits don't live in car boots, JB. No. My bet is it's a headless corpse. Wonder if the thing's unlocked?'

She tried the boot and all the car doors without result, while I peered through the windows. The car was undeniably empty.

'Probably belongs to a couple cuddling somewhere in the woods,' I said. 'Come on, Whisky. Don't be daft.'

Whisky ignored me and continued to paw desperately at the boot.

Then the tapping began.

It was an uneven sort of tapping and it came from inside the boot itself. Three short taps, followed by three long ones, then the three short ones again. There was a pause, then the same sequence was repeated.

'Sounds like something's come loose in there,' I said uneasily.

'N-no.' Polly sounded excited. 'It's morse. Someone's trapped in there. They're tapping SOS.'

We listened. The tapping continued in the same rhythm.

'So they are,' gasped Sam. 'We gotta get them out.'

'How?' I said irritably. 'The thing's locked.'

'I'm a whizz with locks.' Sam whipped out a hair grip from her hair and began to twiddle it about in the boot's lock. We watched tensely. I've seen Sam do this sort of thing before and she's really pretty good at it. In fact, with a bit more practice, she'd make a first rate sidekick for Bill Sikes.

It took her a few minutes before the lock admitted defeat and clicked back. Triumphantly Sam lifted the lid of the boot. Then we froze.

There was a body in the boot. Not a dead one though. A pair of dark eyes in a handsome, black face peered blearily up at us. We stared back, our own eyes round with shock.

The man was dressed in a suit which had once been smart but was now filthy and torn. His hands and feet were bound and he was gagged. Nevertheless, his face looked vaguely familiar. I'd seen him before somewhere. Recently too. Suddenly it dawned on me. But Sam, as usual, had got there first.

'Lordy!' she said in awe. 'It's the Thingummy of Whatsit.'

She was right too. I was sure the man was indeed the same personage we had seen being hurried into the fake embassy car the day before, though he now looked decidedly past his sell-by date.

He began to make urgent noises, looking at us appealingly. Polly said, 'I think he wants that g-gag off.'

Sam was already bending over the boot struggling with the gag. I fished hurriedly in my jeans pocket and produced the really radical penknife I always carry. It's terrific, that knife. It went through the prince's ropes dead easy. In fact at one point I nearly sliced the guy's wrists in my enthusiasm. He didn't complain, just grimaced with

171

pain as feeling began to return to his hands and feet.

'Thank you,' he said politely.

'You *are* the missing prince, aren't you?' said Sam bluntly.

I don't know what she'd have done if the poor guy had said 'No,' since she seemed so set on it. However, he nodded violently before scrambling painfully from his narrow prison.

'We must get away,' he hissed, in surprisingly good English I thought, till I remembered Sam had said he'd been at school in England. 'Before the assassins return we must get away.'

The word 'assassins' made me equally eager to leave. I eyed him doubtfully. He didn't look in very good shape.

'Can you walk?' I said. 'Or perhaps – the car?'

'No keys in the ignition.' Polly was doing his usual wet blanket act.

'I can open the door,' said Sam. 'But—'

'I think I can start the car,' said the prince. 'Something I learned at Harrow,' he added proudly.

'Let's go then,' I said.

Sam was already fiddling with the lock on the driver's door. It didn't defeat her for long. She clambered into the car and opened the other doors.

We piled in.

'Now—' the prince was seated behind the wheel – 'let me see if I can remember . . . .'

He jiggled about with the ignition for a bit. The car gave an apologetic cough or two. We eyed it apprehensively. Then the engine started. It didn't exactly roar into life, mind you. In fact it made a

172

noise like a mouse who could be suffering from a nasty, snuffly cold. But the car began to move. The prince edged it along the track.

'Where are we?' he said. 'And which way do we go?'

'We're in Friary Woods,' I said. 'Where d'you want to go?'

The prince considered this.

'The nearest police station,' he decided. 'My enemies will return soon. With your police I shall be safe.'

'OK,' I said. 'Follow this track till we come out on the road. Then turn right.'

Despite the roughness of the track, the car was now moving quite quickly and the three of us were bouncing about on the back seat. I was just about to suggest a cut in speed when we shot out on to the road.

'Right, you said?' questioned the prince.

'Yeah,' I said.

'Then right again at the end of the lane,' added Sam. 'And that'll bring you on to the main road. There'll be a lot of traffic.'

If this were intended to sound a warning note, the prince ignored it. He was now driving with all the furious, single-minded dedication of a kamikaze pilot. After a minute or two we skidded round the corner on two wheels, cutting in front of a Metro proceeding decorously in the opposite direction.

'Look out!' I yelled.

'It is nice to drive again,' the prince confided. 'I have not driven for years. In my country I am not allowed to drive myself.'

A wise decision, I thought bitterly, while we weaved through the traffic at top speed as if engaged in a motorized version of the downhill slalom.

Suddenly a car going in the opposite direction swerved as it passed us. There were three men in the car, I noticed. Dark skinned they were, like the prince. And they were staring across at us in furious and incredulous recognition.

The prince saw them too.

'The rebels,' he gasped. 'They've seen us.'

Beside me, I heard Polly moan faintly.

Sam was peering out of the back window.

'They've swung round,' she announced. 'They're giving chase.'

The prince muttered something vicious sounding in his own language and stamped on the accelerator. Our vehicle uttered a tortured shriek and leapt forward, almost hitting a bus. The prince swerved wildly, shot past a lorry and, with screaming tyres, skidded round the nearest corner. Polly, I observed, had his eyes tightly shut.

'They're still with us,' reported Sam. 'And gaining.'

Our car swung round to the left, again taking the corner on two wheels, then sprang forward like a Scud missile. I began to feel sick. This sort of chase is great when watched on telly, but I can tell you it's dead scary when you're part of it. Why anyone calls it 'joy riding' I can't imagine. Moreover, our vehicle was now beginning to make peculiar banging noises and the whole thing seemed to be making a determined effort to shake itself to pieces. I had the feeling that the end must come before long.

174

It did too. But not in the way I'd envisaged. Suddenly there came the sound of police sirens. Just ahead of us a cop car shot out of a side road, blocking our path. At the same moment Sam announced, 'There's a carload of cops now behind the baddies.'

After this things began to happen very quickly.

The prince, in an attempt to avoid the police car which was straddled across the road in front of him, swerved violently to the left and wrapped our car round a lamppost. We stopped with a violent jolt which made our freckles rattle. I'd shut my eyes just before the crash, but I heard the sound of another collision and someone yelling, so I opened them to see Polly, his face the leaden hue of suet pudding, clinging to the seat in a way that would have impressed a limpet. Even the usually imperturbable Sam was trembling like a kite in a storm-force wind. Next minute we seemed to be surrounded by cops.

One, wearing a sergeant's stripes on his arm, banged on the window for the prince to open it. He obeyed and beamed at the furious cop.

'Take me at once to your police station,' he commanded.

The sergeant looked a bit taken aback.

'I'm taking you to the police station all right,' he snapped. 'The lot of you. Joy riding at your age! You ought to be ashamed of yourself. Let me see your licence.'

'Licence? I have no licence.' The prince looked bewildered.

'I thought not. *And* this car's been reported stolen. Where did you get it?'

'You are making a mistake.' The prince spoke in tones of liquid ice. 'I am the Crown Prince of—'

'Rubbish!' interrupted the sergeant. 'Joy rider! That's all you are. And encouraging these youngsters to do the same stupid thing. Out of the car the lot of you.'

We scrambled out. The rebels' car, I noticed, had run into the side of one of the police cars and more cops were hauling our pursuers from the wreck.

I pointed towards them.

'Those men,' I said loudly, 'were chasing us. They want to kidnap the prince again. They—'

The sergeant swung round on me.

'And who are you?'

'James Bond,' I said.

The sergeant drew a deep breath. He had turned an unbecoming shade of puce. One of the cops with him said, 'Sarge – d'you think perhaps it's a stunt for some film? You know – for telly?'

'Whatever it is,' said the sergeant heavily, 'we'll sort it out at the station. I'm taking the lot of 'em in. Connors, load this first lot into our car. Price, drive the stolen car back to the nick. And you,' he yelled to the other cops from the rear car, 'bring those three beauties in as well. I'm going to end joy riding in my manor if it kills me.'

'We weren't joy riding,' I said desperately. 'We—'

'Shut up and get in the car,' snapped the sergeant.

We obeyed, followed by Whisky, who flopped

down reproachfully across Polly's feet. The prince, who seemed to be the only one accepting the situation calmly, was shoved ungently into the front passenger seat. At least, I thought, he was likely to be safe from harm for the time being. Even the most dedicated hit man wasn't going to start anything in a cop shop.

After a short and silent drive we arrived at the nick and were hustled inside. A dangerous looking type was standing by the desk talking to a couple of cops.

'No sign of him anywhere,' he was saying. 'We're watching all ports and airports, of course, but I'm afraid he could be out of the country already. Heads'll roll for this, I can tell you.'

'Excuse me,' said our sergeant loudly. 'Could I come through with these joy riders for questioning?'

The three men turned to face us. Then the plain clothes guy did a sort of double take and leapt forward.

'Your Highness,' he gasped. 'You're safe. They found you.'

'No,' corrected the prince gently. 'These children found me. The police, for some reason, have arrested me. And those three,' he gestured towards the unhappy rebels who had just been marched in, 'are trying to abduct me.'

'I see,' said Plain Clothes, in a tone which revealed he didn't see at all. 'I suggest we find an interview room somewhere and sort things out. I'll just get on the blower and say you've been found.'

'I must insist,' said the prince sternly, 'that those three assassins are put in a cell at once.'

'Yes. Do that, will you?' Plain Clothes told our sergeant abruptly.

'But—' began the sergeant.

'Just do it,' snapped Plain Clothes irritably. 'I'll explain later.'

'Sir!' The sergeant, obviously beginning to see his dreams of speedy promotion fading, hurried to obey.

After that things began to sort themselves out quite nicely. We were taken, together with the prince, to a room which appeared to be the nearest thing the nick had to a VIP suite, where we were given tea and sandwiches and things. Plain Clothes type had, by this time, been joined by two similar models, plus a uniformed guy wearing a lot of gold braid and the manner to go with it. Then the prince described how he'd been snatched and drugged and shoved into the car boot.

'Tonight,' he said, 'I was to have been packed into a crate and loaded on a boat to be taken back to my own country. If these three brave children hadn't rescued me I should have had no hope of survival.'

Gold Braid turned to us.

'How did you find him?'

'It was Whisky really,' I said. 'That's Whisky there. He was pawing at the boot of the car. Then we heard the prince tapping SOS, so—'

'So I forced the lock,' said Sam brightly.

Between us we went through the whole story, including the upside down flag bit. Both the prince and Gold Braid seemed pretty impressed.

'You're three very resourceful young people,'

Gold Braid told us. 'And we're very grateful. Now we're going to have you taken safely home in a police car. And you, sir,' he turned to the prince, 'will be taken to a safe house, where you can stay for the time being.'

'Thank you,' said the prince politely. 'And will it be possible for me to have a bath and a change of clothes?'

Gold Braid grinned.

'I think we can run to that, sir.'

The prince turned to us.

'I can never thank you enough,' he said. 'You, James Bond, and your friends. If all goes well in my country I shall remember.'

So he shook hands with each of us – including Whisky. It was one of those dramatic moments where you almost expect to hear about fifty violins going berserk in the background.

Over the next week or so the three of us glued ourselves to all the news bulletins on telly to see what was happening in the prince's country. Finally we heard that the uprising had been defeated and its leaders duly imprisoned. On the news next evening we saw the prince arriving back in his own country, to the cheers of his loyal people.

'Well, that's that,' said Polly. He and I were watching telly on his own private set in that luxury bed-sit his doting oldies have bestowed on him. 'D'you think we'll get a reward?'

'Should do,' I said. 'The guy's stinking rich, isn't he? Probably get a grand each at least.'

It was a few days later that a large, flat parcel was delivered, addressed to me. It contained a very nice typewritten letter, signed by the Crown Prince himself, thanking us for our service to his country. The package also contained a sort of scroll thing in weird writing and a foreign language, together with three medals which looked like they might be gold. I hurried round to Sam with our prize, then we both pelted over to Polly's pad to put him in the picture.

'Of course, cash would have been great,' I said. 'But we can't half swank round school with these medals. Fatso Austin and his mob'll be livid.'

'Yeah,' said Sam. 'I think it's megacool. The Vigilantes have really proved themselves on this one.'

'Dead right,' I said. 'Lucky I thought of the idea of us being vigilantes in the first place, wasn't it?'

I saw Sam looking at me in that cool, haughty, scornful way she has.

'Actually, JB,' she said coldly, '*I* was the one who thought of it. Remember?'

'Here, hang on,' I said, 'I—'

'But,' interrupted Polly, 'I thought of the name "Vigilantes". And it was me spotted that flag was upside down, wasn't it?'

'Well,' I said, 'I was just—'

'And,' continued Polly blithely, 'it was my dog that found the car and—'

'I was going—' I began.

Polly overrode me.

'*And* I was the one who realized it was SOS being tapped on the boot. I think I've done jolly well.'

'Yeah – well – OK,' I said grudgingly. 'Seems like my training's paying off at last.'

Polly glared at me indignantly. Sam smiled her Mona Lisa Mark 2 smile. My lieutenants, I thought, were getting altogether too uppity for their own good. I silently determined to cut them down to size before we were plunged into any more adventures.

Join the RED FOX Reader's Club

The Red Fox Readers' Club is for readers of all ages. All you have to do is ask your local bookseller or librarian for a Red Fox Reader's Club card. As an official Red Fox Reader you will qualify for your own Red Fox Reader's Clubpack – full of exciting surprises! If you have any difficulty obtaining a Red Fox Readers' Club card please write to: Random House Children's Books Marketing Department, 20 Vauxhall Bridge Road, London SW1V 2SA.

Other great reads from **Red Fox**

Further Red Fox titles that you might enjoy reading are listed on the following pages. They are available in bookshops or they can be ordered directly from us.

If you would like to order books, please send this form and the money due to:

ARROW BOOKS, BOOKSERVICE BY POST, PO BOX 29, DOUGLAS, ISLE OF MAN, BRITISH ISLES. Please enclose a cheque or postal order made out to Arrow Books Ltd for the amount due, plus 75p per book for postage and packing to a maximum of £7.50, both for orders within the UK. For customers outside the UK, please allow £1.00 per book.

NAME_____

ADDRESS_____

_____

Please print clearly.

Whilst every effort is made to keep prices low, it is sometimes necessary to increase cover prices at short notice. If you are ordering books by post, to save delay it is advisable to phone to confirm the correct price. The number to ring is THE SALES DEPARTMENT 071 (if outside London) 973 9700.

Other great reads ✈ *from* **Red Fox**

Chocks Away with Biggles!

Squadron-Leader James Bigglesworth – better known to his fans as Biggles – has been thrilling millions of readers all over the world with all his amazing adventures for many years. Now Red Fox are proud to have reissued a collection of some of Captain W. E. Johns' most exciting and fast-paced stories about the flying Ace, in brand-new editions, guaranteed to entertain young and old readers alike.

BIGGLES LEARNS TO FLY
ISBN 0 09 999740 1   £3.50

BIGGLES FLIES EAST
ISBN 0 09 993780 8   £3.50

BIGGLES AND THE RESCUE FLIGHT
ISBN 0 09 993860 X   £3.50

BIGGLES OF THE FIGHTER SQUADRON
ISBN 0 09 993870 7   £3.50

BIGGLES & CO.
ISBN 0 09 993800 6   £3.50

BIGGLES IN SPAIN
ISBN 0 09 913441 1   £3.50

BIGGLES DEFIES THE SWASTIKA
ISBN 0 09 993790 5   £3.50

BIGGLES IN THE ORIENT
ISBN 0 09 913461 6   £3.50

BIGGLES DEFENDS THE DESERT
ISBN 0 09 993840 5   £3.50

BIGGLES FAILS TO RETURN
ISBN 0 09 993850 2   £3.50